Frank Cottrell-Boyce

CAN A DOG FROM OUTER SPACE SAVE THE WORLD?

SPUTNIK'S GUIDE TO LIFE ON EARTH

Illustrated by Steven Lenton

MACMILLAN

First published 2016 by Macmillan Children's Books

This edition published 2019 by Macmillan Children's Books
an imprint of Pan Macmillan
The Smithson, 6 Briset Street, London EC1M 5NR
Associated companies throughout the world
www.panmacmillan.com

ISBN 978-1-5290-0881-4

5 7 9 8 6

A CIP catalogue record for this book is available from
the British Library.

Printed and bound by CPI Group (UK) Ltd, Croydon CR0 4YY

For Keziah and Samuel – the beloved children of Christiana Eke Adah

Before you start anything, make a list. That's what my grandad says. If you're making a cake, make a list. If you're moving house, make a list. If you're running away to sea, make a list.

At least, that's what he used to say. Nowadays who knows what he's going to say? Sometimes he looks in the mirror and says, 'Who's a bonnie boy then, eh?' Sometimes he looks in the mirror and shouts, 'Who's this old bod in my mirror?! What's he doing in my bedroom?'

Sometimes he comes into the kitchen and says, 'Tickets, please!'

And it's no good saying, 'Grandad, you're not on a ship any more. This is the kitchen. I don't need a ticket,' because that just gets him going.

If he asks for a ticket, I just look in my pocket for a piece of paper, hand it over and wait to see what he does.

Usually it's 'That seems to be in order. Take a seat and enjoy your voyage'. Then he gives you a little salute and you salute him back.

Sometimes it's 'This is a second-class ticket, not valid in this part of the ship'. Then I have to go out into the sitting room, wait a bit and come back in again.

Today was a 'Tickets, please!' day, so I handed him the red notebook I was holding, open as though it was my passport. I said, 'I think you'll find this is in order.'

1. Spicy Chicken Wings
2. 28 June - Annabel's Birthday
3. Lightsabers
4. Mooring Hitch Knots
5. Laika
6. The Companion
7. 1kg Plain Flour, 1 Tub Margarine, 500g Mushrooms
8. Milk
9. Chicken-and-Mushroom Pie
10. Spanish Lessons
11. Eggs
12. Concealer

13. Post-It Notes
14. 31 July – St Peter's Summer Treat
15. TV Remote Control
16. Curtains
17. Jailbreak
18. Geese
19. Be Nice
20. Spaghetti
21. Fire Drill
22. Shangri-La
23. Stairlift
24. Teeth
25. Grandad's Harmonica
26. Postcards
27. The Sea Chest

He gave it the hard stare.

Then he gave me the hard stare.

'I know a list when I see one,' he said, 'and this –' he shoved it back into my hand – 'is just a shopping list. Mostly.'

'Now that,' I said, 'is where you're wrong. '*This* is a list of all the startling things that happened this summer.'

'What happened this summer?'

'Read it and see. I probably shouldn't have written it all down. It might get me into trouble. We broke a lot of laws, including some of the laws of physics. But I wrote everything down anyway because I didn't want to forget any of it.'

1.
Spicy Chicken Wings

I don't know why I answered the door.

It wasn't even my own door.

By then I was staying at the Children's Temporary Accommodation, but in the summer they put you with a family. They put me on a farm called Stramoddie with a family called the Blythes. It's right down near Knockbrex.

When Mrs Rowland from the Temporary dropped me off, she said, 'This is Prez. He's a good boy but he doesn't talk much. He's very helpful, but perhaps best not to let him near your kitchen knives.'

'When you say he doesn't talk . . .'

'Hasn't said a word in months.'

'Just exactly what we need,' said the dad. 'Someone to balance out our Jessie. Jessie does enough talking for ten families.'

That's one good thing about not talking, by the way – you don't have to work out what to call the mum and dad. You can't call them Mum and Dad, because they're *not* your mum or your dad. Calling them Mr and Mrs Whatever would be weird. And calling them by their first names is even weirder.

'Even if you did want to speak, Prez, you wouldn't get a word in. This is the House of Blether.'

He was not joking. Mostly they talk so much and so loud, you can't tell who's saying what. Though mostly it's Jessie.

'Everyone to the kitchen!'

'Wait a minute!'

'No! No more minutes, we've waited long enough.'

'I hate baked potatoes.'

'Say hello to Prez.'

'Who's Prez? Oh. Hi.'

'It's not a restaurant.'

'I hate sitting here.'

'No phones at the dinner table!'

Then they all drop their heads and say a prayer very quietly. But the second they've said amen, they all start shouting again.

'Ray, do not reach for the water. Ask someone to pass it!'

'Prez, that big boy is Ray, the little girl is Annabel and this is Jessie . . .'

'He's staying for the summer. He normally lives with his grandad but . . .'

'Why do you live with your grandad? Why don't you live with your mother?'

'Prez doesn't like to talk.'

'Why doesn't he like to talk?'

'He's not allowed near knives.'

'Some people just do live with their grandads, that's all. Not everyone lives with their mum.'

'Why aren't you allowed knives? Did you stab someone?'

'Jessie, it's really rude to ask people if they've ever stabbed people.'

Folk think that if you're not talking you're not listening. But that's not true. For instance, I was the only one who heard the doorbell the night that Sputnik came.

It was a Wednesday. Tea was spicy chicken wings, salad and baked potatoes. We'd finished eating and everyone was clearing up in the kitchen.

The doorbell rang.

The family didn't hear it because they were all shouting.

'Why is
everyone shouting?'

'The radio's too loud.
We have to shout to be heard.'

'No. The radio is loud so
I can hear it over the shouting.
If there wasn't shouting,
the radio would be quiet.'

The doorbell rang again.

I never answer doors, because answering doors means you have to speak to someone, sometimes a stranger even.

The doorbell rang again.

Then I thought, What if it's my grandad?!

I used to live with my grandad, but he got into a wee spot of bother and had to be taken away. That's how I ended up in the Children's Temporary. They said that if Grandad could get himself sorted out, he would be allowed to come back and I could go and live with him again.

Maybe this was Grandad – all sorted out and coming to take me back to the flat in Traquair Gardens.

Maybe I was going home.

So I answered the door.

But it wasn't Grandad. It was Sputnik.

I have to describe him because there's a lot of disagreement about what he looks like:

Height and age – about the same as me.

Clothes – unusual. For instance: slightly-too-big jumper, kilt, leather helmet like the ones pilots wear in war movies, with massive goggles.

Weapons – a massive pair of scissors stuffed into

his belt like a sword. There were other weapons but I didn't know about them then or I definitely wouldn't have let him in.

Luggage – a big yellow backpack. I now know he more or less never takes that backpack off.

Name – Sputnik, though that's not what he said to start with.

Manners – not good. My grandad always says that good manners are important. 'Good manners tell you what to do when you don't know what to do,' he says. Sputnik put his hand out to me, so I shook it. That's good manners. But Sputnik did not shake back. Instead Sputnik grabbed my hand with both of his and swung himself in through the door, using my arms like a rope.

'Mellows?' he said.

Mellows is my second name. So I thought, This must be someone from the Temporary coming to take me back. Maybe Grandad had got himself sorted out. Maybe the family have complained about me.

'I too . . .' he said, pushing his goggles up on to the top of his head, 'am the Mellows.' He thumped his chest. It sounded like a drum.

Oh. We had the same name.

'The same name!' He flung his arms around me. I don't know much about hugs, but if a hug is so fierce it makes you worry that your lungs might pop out through your nostrils, that's a big hug.

I didn't know what to do. The Blythes were noisy, but I was pretty sure they'd notice if I let a stranger in goggles and a kilt into their front room. They seemed easy-going enough, but it had to be against the rules just to let any old stranger walk into the house.

'Stranger!' he said, as though he had heard what I was thinking. 'Stranger! Where's the stranger?! We have the same name. We. Are. Family!'

He strolled right past me, pulling his goggles back down.

The mum was in the living room about to turn the TV on, with her back to the door. Mellows put his hands on his hips and yelled, 'I. Am. Starving! Take me to your larder!' The mum spun round, dropped the remote, stared at him, then stared at me. I thought she was going to scream. But she didn't.

She smiled the biggest smile I'd ever seen her smile and she said, 'Ooohhhh, aren't you lovely?!'

'Yes,' said Mellows, 'I *am* lovely. Let the loveliness begin for the lovely one is here!' Then he actually sang, 'Here comes the Mellows!' to the tune of The Beatles' 'Here Comes the Sun'.

The mum looked at me and said, 'Is he lost?' She didn't wait for me to answer. 'Everyone, come and see!' The entire family avalanched into the living room.

'Amazing!' yelled Jessie. 'Did Dad bring him?'

'No. Prez did.'

'Prez? Really?'

'Nice one, Prez.'

Maybe I'd done the right thing.

Mellows strode over and shook Jessie's hand.

Jessie shouted, 'Whoa! Did you see that? He shook hands with me!' She seemed to think shaking hands was a rare and unusual thing, like walking on water or having hair made of snakes.

Annabel waddled past Jessie, saying, 'Me now, me now.' She shook hands with him and they all clapped.

Don't get me wrong. When Mrs Rowland brought me down to Stramoddie, they were all really nice to me. The food was way better than in the Temporary, Ray let me have the top bunk, they gave me my own pair of wellies for walking around the farm, but nobody actually clapped. There was no fighting over whose turn it was to shake hands with me! And no one did what Jessie did to Mellows. She called him a 'bonnie wee man' and she rubbed noses with him!

The mum asked him if he was hungry.

'Got it in one!' roared Mellows. 'That's why I said, "Take me to your larder!" Do it now before I starve to death before your very eyes!'

He flung himself on to the floor as though he was dying there and then. The mum ran into the kitchen and came back with the leftover spicy chicken wings. If you're going to eat food, it's good manners to get a plate and a knife and fork and sit down. Unless it's chips. You can eat chips in the park. But the mum did not give Mellows a knife and fork or a plate or a place at the table. No. She held a spicy chicken wing up in the air. Mellows looked up at it. Then she dropped the chicken right into his mouth. He chewed and sucked at it, then pulled the clean bones out of his mouth.

Not good manners.

I think if I'd done that people would have complained. When Mellows did it, they didn't complain. They clapped again.

The mum said he was a clever boy!

'No doubt about that,' said Mellows. 'I *am* a clever boy. I'm a chuffing genius if the truth be told.'

When the dad came in and saw Mellows sprawled on the couch, Jessie said, 'Can he stay? Can he stay? Please can he stay?'

'I suppose so,' said the dad with a big sigh. 'But just for tonight.'

'Shake hands with him!'

The dad shook hands with Mellows and asked him his name. Then he asked him his name again, like, 'What's his name? What's his name? What's his name?'

Mellows pleaded with me to make him stop.

'Please tell this joker my name before he shakes my hand off!'

Before I could stop myself I said, 'Mellows,' out loud.

Everyone stared at me.

'Yes! I am Mellows,' said Mellows. He pointed at me. 'Two merits for listening skills.'

No one looked at Mellows. They were all still staring at me.

'Mellows?' said the mum. 'Like you, Prez? That's lovely. Well done, Prez.'

I knew she meant, Well done for talking.

Until the night Sputnik came, I used to lie on the top bunk in Ray's room every night, looking at the ceiling and worrying about Grandad. When Grandad used to go off on his big long walks, for instance, I always went after him to make sure he didn't get lost. Who would go after him now? Maybe he wasn't even allowed to go off any more? Maybe they locked him in?

But after Sputnik came I didn't have time to think about anything but Sputnik. That first night, for instance, I was thinking . . . Sputnik rang the doorbell. But there is no front doorbell at Stramoddie.

2.
28 June – Annabel's Birthday

One thing that made me feel good when I came to Stramoddie was the lists. They put lists everywhere. They had a shopping list on the fridge door.

A 'Whose Turn It Is To Do What' list on the kitchen noticeboard.

Post-it notes about food on the kitchen table.

A whiteboard with 'Every Single Morning' written on it:

> Empty dishwasher
> Feed chickens
> Turn out ponies
> Check gates
> Switch on cow crossing

It had a Sharpie stuck to it so you could put a tick next to each thing when you'd done it.

Grandad used to be a cook on a ship. 'I've cooked for kings and criminals on all the Seven Seas,' he liked to say. 'One thing I know is, life is like cooking. Before you start, make a list. That way you know where you're up to.' He also says, 'Make yourself useful. Life is like a kitchen. If you stand around doing nothing, someone is bound to spill something hot on you.'

Those first days, I didn't know how to make myself useful with chickens or ponies. But I did know how to empty a dishwasher so I did that every morning. And checking the calendar reminded me of being back at Traquair Gardens with Grandad, so I did that every morning too. That's how I knew that the day after Sputnik arrived was Annabel's fifth birthday.

Annabel's Party List
Friends arrive
Musical Bumps/Statues
Pass the Parcel
Musical Chairs
Presents
Food
Playing Out
Cake

Presents. I didn't want to be the only one not giving her a present. The nearest shops to Stramoddie are about a million miles away, at Kirkcudbright. I thought I could make her a card and maybe find something in my backpack that I could wrap up for her. I just needed some paper and scissors.

The others were putting up a 'Happy Birthday' banner in the kitchen and laying out bowls of snacks. The only one who wasn't helping was Mellows. He was sprawled on the couch with his hands behind his head. I noticed the scissors in his belt.

'Want to borrow them?' he said.

– That would be good.

'No problem.' Without even looking at me, he swiped the scissors out of his belt and flung them across the room. They flashed through the air and stuck, shivering, deep in the wood of the door, right next to my head.

I held my breath.

'I never miss.' He grinned. 'Unless I mean to. What are you going to give her?'

– I'm not sure yet.

'Food. Everyone loves food. Just give her food.'

– She has loads of food. They're laying it out in the kitchen. There's a bowl of Hula Hoops in there you could swim in.

'Let's go! Let's swim!'

– No. I've got to go and get her a present.

He followed me up to Ray's bedroom. I keep everything in my backpack. I never unpack. I emptied all my stuff on to the bed to see if I had anything that would make a good present for little Annabel.

'You know,' said Mellows, looking out of the window, 'this is an excellent little planet. You're crazy to think of running away.'

– How do you know I'm thinking of running away?

'Your bag is packed. Including your toothbrush. You might as well be wearing an "I'm Thinking of Running Away from Home" T-shirt.'

– But this isn't my home. I'm just a visitor. If I ran away, I'd be running *back* home. I keep my bag packed in case something goes wrong and I get sent back to the Children's Temporary. Hang on – this is like we're having a conversation. But I'm not talking.

'I'm reading your mind. If you won't speak, you leave me no choice but to read your mind.'

– You can read minds?

'I can do things you haven't dreamed of. Can't you feel me in your mind? Like someone tickling the inside of your skull with a toothbrush?'

– That's exactly what it feels like. Stop it.

'Oh, but I'm having such a nice time inside your head. How about these? I bet little Annabel would love these!'

– Those are my underpants.

'Sorry. Such bright colours. Thought they were some kind of tortilla. Are you sure they're not edible?'

– They're definitely not edible.

'What about this?'

– That's the chopping knife my grandad gave me. It's really sharp. It's exactly the same as his. No one's supposed to know I've got it. Give it back.

'Whoa – look at these! Do you know the people in these pictures?'

– They're my Star Wars Top Trumps cards.

'I'd love to meet this guy. He looks so nice – all smooth and shiny.'

– That's Darth Vader. He's the incarnation of evil. You're a rotten judge of character.

'I bet if I met him I could find his good side.'

– He's not real.

'How can you have a photo of someone who's not real?' He was jangling my set of keys with the Leaning Tower of Pisa key ring.

– They're the keys to the flat in Traquair. We'll be going back there as soon as Grandad gets sorted.

'This?'

– A used train ticket from the time we went to Glasgow and got lost.

'This?'

– That's Grandad's harmonica. He used to play it when he was all alone on the night watch up on deck. He was playing that when he spotted the iceberg.

Mellows blew into it randomly. It wheezed and squeaked. 'That,' he said, 'is what I call music. Can I have it?'

– No. It's Grandad's.

'OK. What's that?'

– That's my map. It's important. Put it down.

'What's it a map of?'

– Places we went together when I was a wean. He drew it for me. Put it back.

Then I had a thought . . .

– Hey. You rang on the doorbell yesterday.

'Yeah.'

– But there is no doorbell.

'That's right.'

– . . .

'I always carry a doorbell with me. Just in case.' He rooted around in his yellow backpack and pulled out an electric doorbell with great lengths of wire hanging out of it.

– Right. So, what else have you got in *your* backpack?

'My backpack? No, no. You won't find a present in here. Everything in here is crucial to my survival. Or my research.'

He rooted through my stuff and pulled out something else.

– Oh, that was a present. Ages ago.

'A present. Exactly what you're looking for!'

It was an old plastic lightsaber that Grandad got me the time we went to Glasgow, the kind with a plastic blade that telescopes out when you flick it.

'She'll love it. Let's wrap it up.'

It was a red one, like for a Sith or Darth Maul. A green one – like for Yoda – would have been better for a five-year-old, but that was all I had.

By the time we went to bed that night I wished I'd been more careful in my choice of lightsaber.

Friends Arrive

I'd never seen a children's birthday party up close before. On my birthdays it was always just me and Grandad. He'd make me a cake. Usually one shaped like a pirate ship. 'I've baked cakes for kings and criminals in all the Seven Seas. Make a wish and blow the candles out.' He used to say that every birthday. Annabel's cake was on a table in the corner. It was shaped like Angelina Ballerina. There was too much pink icing and it all wobbled worryingly once Annabel's little mates started tumbling into the room.

'Everyone,' said the mum, when Annabel's friends arrived, 'this is Prez Mellows and this is . . . Mr Mellows.'

'Where did this lot all come from? Have they had more children in the night?' said Mellows.

– They're Annabel's friends. Be nice to them.

So Mellows shook hands with the nearest little girl. She shrieked with happiness. Then the next one wanted to shake his hand too and hordes of little Disney princesses were more or less wrestling with each other for the chance to shake hands with Mellows.

None of them was even a tiny bit interested in shaking hands with me.

Musical Bumps, Statues, Chairs, etc.

Then the music started and the little Disney princesses started jumping up and down in time to 'Let It Go'. The music stopped. They all stood dead still.

'We're playing musical statues,' said Jessie. 'Want a shot in charge of the music, Prez? You just press pause or play whenever you feel like it.'

It was a chance to make myself useful.

Mellows came and stood next to me. 'This is just incredible,' he said. 'What we have here is push-button children. How does it work? Are they robots? Droids? Hypnotized?'

– No, it's just a game. See? I press stop and they stop.

I pressed stop and they stopped.

– I press play and they start.

I pressed play and they started.

'Can you make them go faster?'

– I suppose.

I switched from 'Let It Go' to 'Hakuna Matata', and the princesses all started jumping up and down like wallabies waiting for the toilet.

Mellows grinned. 'Perfect.'

Then I slowed it right down to 'Do You Want to Build a Snowman?'.

Jessie declared me the best musical-statues DJ ever. I stayed in charge of the music for musical chairs and pass the parcel.

Presents

Annabel loved the lightsaber! She threw her arms around my middle and shouted, 'Mum! I got a magic wand!'

'That's actually a lightsaber,' said Jessie.

'It does magic,' insisted Annabel. She kept shaking the blade out and tipping it back in again, even when they were eating their pizzas.

'Great present, Prez,' said Ray.

One of Annabel's friends – the one with the blonde ponytail who doesn't come any more because of what happened next – pointed out that the lightsaber didn't work.

'Given that it's a deadly weapon, that's probably a good thing,' said the dad.

Food, Cake etc.

Even though they'd given Mellows plenty to eat, he still seemed to mainly be interested in food. He watched over the big bowl of Hula Hoops like it was a sleeping baby. When the mum brought in the Angelina Ballerina birthday cake, you would have thought the cake was a massive magnet and his eyes were little iron marbles. I really thought they would pop right out of his head. He was hypnotized by that cake.

The mum spotted him licking his lips and said, 'Prez. Wee job for you. Would you take Mellows for a walk?'

– Take him for a walk? Why would I take him for a walk? Why wouldn't he just *go* for a walk?

'I think he's probably hungry, but I don't want him near the food until the children have eaten. Just in case. If you know what I mean?'

I had no idea what she meant.

Jessie came running up. 'I'll take him out,' she said. 'I want to take him out.'

But Mellows wouldn't budge. 'I can't believe you're trying to throw me out when there's food. You know I love food.'

'Come on, Mellows,' said Jessie. Then: 'He won't move.' She tried pushing him. I mean, pushing someone out the door – how is that manners? I didn't know what else to do so I walked out into the farmyard.

Mellows followed me.

'Prez has got the knack,' said the mum.

'Thanks for that, Mum,' said Jessie.

One side of the farmyard is a big whitewashed barn with no windows, where they keep the tractors and the calves. There's a little grassy bit with a fence around it, full of chickens. Then there's a row of stables with those doors that only go halfway up. Two of them have got ponies in but they belong to the neighbours so you can't ride them. You can give them carrots though. And Jessie gets to take them out into the paddock in the mornings. Just now the ponies were standing with their heads poking over the stable doors, as if they were hanging them out to dry. Jessie ran past us saying, 'Mellows, come here! Come here. Come here and see.'

She went to the empty stable at the end and opened the door. Someone had cleaned the stall out. There was a massive tartan cushion in the corner, some kind of washing basket with a blanket in it, a ball and a bowl of water. The dad was inside, fixing a sign to the door with a drill and some screws.

'What do you think?' he asked when Mellows looked in.

– I think it's a stall with a cushion, a ball and a bowl of water in.

That was what *I* thought.

Mellows took a deep breath. 'Creosote,' he said, 'a little tang of hedgehog wee, chicken droppings and WD-40. It's got good smells. It's earthy. It's masculine. It's very me. I love it.'

'It's all yours.' The dad smiled. 'You'll be much happier here than in the house. You don't have to wait for someone to let you out if you want to run around a bit. Out here, you've got your freedom.'

– Wait. Are they saying they want you to *sleep* out here? In a stable?!

'Of course,' said the dad. 'It's only temporary. Until we find your real home.'

'Temporary,' whooped Annabel, who had followed Mellows out and was now hugging my leg. 'Like Prez!' she squealed, running back inside.

'What does he mean, real home?' asked Mellows.

– You know. Somewhere you came from. Somewhere you live.

'I live wherever I am. I live all over the place. Always moving. Like your grandad.'

– How do you know about my grandad?

'I know he was a sailor.'

– But he came from somewhere. He belonged somewhere.

'I belong,' said Mellows, 'to the universe. All of it. This stable or the back of Betelgeuse, it's all the same to me.'

'Look!' Jessie smiled. 'I made this.'

She pointed to the sign that the dad had now finished screwing to the doorpost. It said 'Mr Mellows' in neat red letters on a piece of wood.

'Oh, please,' said Mellows, 'we're friends now. Call me Sputnik. Sputnik is my first name.'

'Sputnik?!' I was so surprised I said this out loud, like, 'SPUTNIK?!'

Jessie stared at me.

The dad stared at me.

Then they stared at each other.

Then they stared at me again.

Finally they said, 'Sput-nik?' both together.

'Perfect,' said Sputnik. 'It's Russian. It means "companion" in English.'

'Are you saying his name is Sputnik?' said the dad. 'Only you did tell us it was Mellows.'

I said 'Sputnik' again.

'You've only said two words since you arrived,' said Jessie. 'Two words, and you've still managed to contradict yourself.'

'If you say Sputnik, Prez,' said the dad, 'then Sputnik it is. Maybe Jess could make a new sign after the party.'

'Sputnik Mellows,' I said.

'Oh!' said the dad. 'Sputnik Mellows! I see. Sputnik Mellows.' He said it a few times, like he was trying to taste it. 'So he's got a first name *and* a second name?'

– Of course he's got a first name and a second name. Everyone has.

'Sputnik Mellows. I like it. So you don't have to make a new sign after all, Jess. Just have to put an *S* in between the Mr and the Mellows. Mr S. Mellows. See?'

'First time I've heard of a dog with a surname,' said Jessie.

DOG?! What was she talking about? *Dog?!* Who was she calling a dog?

That's when it clicked.

People pat Sputnik on the head.

People drop food in his mouth.

People tell him he's a good boy.

They're amazed when he shakes hands.

And now Jessie was on tiptoe holding a chunk of chocolate high above Sputnik's head, saying, 'Come on, boy, beg, beg.'

Sputnik raised an eyebrow. 'Why would I beg for chocolate? If I wanted chocolate, I'd go and buy some.'

– Sputnik, this is really strange and probably sounds really rude, but I think the whole family has mistaken you for a dog.

'Ah.' Sputnik smiled. 'That explains everything.'

– No, no. It doesn't explain anything. Why would they think you were a dog?

'Think about it. Humans and dogs share ninety per cent of their DNA. Biologically they're practically the same thing. Obviously people are going to make mistakes from time to time.'

– Is that true?! Ninety per cent the same DNA? That's bananas!

'Humans also share fifty per cent of their DNA,' he said, 'with bananas.'

– No!

'Besides –' he shrugged – 'I'm Sputnik Mellows. Sputnik Mellows does not care what people think.'

– But if you look like a dog to everyone else, how come you look like a human being to me?

'Because you . . .' said Sputnik, 'you are the whole point of my mission.'

– Your *mission*?

'Everyone in the universe has a mission. You're mine.'

3.
Lightsabers

Before Sputnik could tell me any more, the dad took me and Jessie out into the yard 'for a quiet word'. I had to go, because if you're a visitor you have to do as you're told.

'A few rules,' he said, 'about Sputnik. Are you listening?'

Jessie said yes. I nodded.

'First of all – not in the house. This is a farm. If he stays . . .'

'He is staying, isn't he?'

'. . . as long as no one claims him. I'm going to make enquiries on the caravan site just in case he's someone's pet.'

'He hasn't got a collar on.'

'I know. So. If he does stay, then he's a farm dog, not a pet. So he belongs out here in his kennel, not in the house.'

'What if it's cold?'

'He can come into the kitchen, that's all. Second, and much, much more important, this is a dairy farm. I can't have him frightening the beasts. If you two want him to stay, then you two have to teach him how to behave around cattle. OK? You have to train him. You have to keep an eye on him.'

'Yes, fine,' said Jessie. I nodded again.

'It's a big responsibility, but it's your responsibility.'

Playing Out

Because she was the birthday girl, Annabel was the first one outside. She went tumbling across the yard with her lightsaber in her chubby little hand. Her friends all came behind her, skipping and screaming, the plastic diamonds on their big floaty dresses twinkling in the sun.

'These children,' said Sputnik, 'they're very . . . pink and shiny. Like icing.'

– That's just their party clothes.

'Are they edible?'

– *No!* They're not edible. They're really not edible.

'Are you sure? They look edible.'

– They are *not* edible. Do not bite them.

Ray brought the last children outside, shouting, 'Annabel! Look what I found under my bed!' He waved a green plastic lightsaber over his head. 'Who wants a lightsaber duel?'

'Me!' whooped Annabel. She came straight for Ray and clobbered his virtuous lightsaber with her evil one.

'Ow!' Ray dropped his lightsaber.

The little girl with the blonde ponytail grabbed it. The two little girls had a Yoda versus Darth Maul duel up and down the yard. They had to be moved because they were worrying the ponies. All the kids were chivvied into the garden. Annabel managed to get up on top of a wheelbarrow and disarm her friend just by the shed.

Then she waggled her own lightsaber in Sputnik's face and threw it – not very far because she was only little – shouting, 'Go on, Sputnik! Fetch!'

Sputnik looked at me. 'Fetch? Is she serious? Fetch? Really?!'

– She thinks you're a dog, remember. Go on. She's only wee.

'Sputnik Mellows does not fetch.'

– It's her birthday.

'Just. This. Once.' He trotted over to the lightsaber and examined it. 'You said this was a lightsaber. It doesn't do anything. It's broken.'

– I think it needs batteries. She doesn't mind. She likes it.

'Have you got the manual?'

– It's just a toy. Go on. Fetch it for her.

'I won't fetch,' said Sputnik. 'Fetching is beneath me. What I will do is fix it.' He fiddled around with it for a while, then handed it to Annabel.

Annabel's-Friend-Who-We-Don't-See-Any-More came at her with the green lightsaber. Annabel whooped and shook her lightsaber. A telescopic plastic blade should have popped out, but it didn't. Instead, a column of blinding, buzzing, red light sliced the air.

Everyone stared.

– Wow, you really did make it work!

'I am the Sputnik.'

Annabel's friend swiped at her with her plastic lightsaber. Annabel parried. The friend's lightsaber exploded in a thick black cloud of stinking smoke. Melted plastic dripped down the handle. The friend squealed with delight. Annabel squealed with even more delight.

– Oh! Hang on, this could be really dangerous.

'Yes. It could!' Sputnik said with a smile, as though really dangerous was the best thing a birthday party could ever be. 'They'll remember this for a long time.'

Annabel tore around the garden with the Darth Maul lightsaber, looking for stuff to destroy. She started with the wheelbarrow. Hot yellow sparks fireworked from the metal as she swung the blade. The handle fell smoking on to the grass. Her friends screamed and begged for more. They didn't seem to be worried that they might be next after the wheelbarrow. They chased after her when she ran at the sheet of corrugated metal that was holding up the compost heap. It

is not wise to run under a climbing frame while waving a fully functioning lightsaber over your head. It will definitely cut the monkey bars in half and slam the jagged ends into the grass. The kids jumped back. They howled with laughter. They seemed to think being nearly impaled by a smouldering monkey bar was the most fun you could ever have.

Destruction! They loved it!

They clapped while Annabel melted the corrugated metal. They cheered as the drips rolled down its ripples like ice cream. 'More! More!'

Annabel swung around to take a bow. Her best friend, a little girl in a *Frozen* costume, saw the blade of light coming towards her and ducked just in time to stop it decapitating her. But not in time to save her thick blonde ponytail, which fell at her feet like a dead gerbil that was slightly on fire. Everyone stared at it in horrible silence.

It could have cut her head off.

'Said I could fix it, didn't I?' said Sputnik, smiling more than ever. 'Smell that burning hair! This is a great party.'

– We have to stop this. Someone could get killed.

'Why give her a lightsaber if you don't want her to use it?!'

– It's supposed to light up and twinkle! Not cut things in half!

'Twinkle? Where's the fun in twinkling?! This is a fantastic party. I was told Earth parties were good, but I never realized they'd be *this* good. I never realized they'd involve so much fire and destruction. These kids are having a great time.'

He was right about that. Having your hair cut by a fully functioning lightsaber was the new face-painting. A little girl held her pigtails out straight while Annabel slashed at them. A girl with a massive Afro stood with her eyes closed and let Annabel shave it all off in a confetti of hot sparks.

– Can't you get the lightsaber off her?

'Are you asking me to fetch again?! Sputnik does not fetch. Oh! Get a lungful of that! That is true perfume. You could bottle that and sell it. Burning hair, hot sawdust and smouldering bark. Aaaahhhh.'

– Bark?

At the corner of the yard, next to the big gate that opens on to the field, there was a big, twisted tree. It must have been there since before the farmhouse was built. Its lowest branch was higher than the roof. Its highest was somewhere out of sight in a cloud of leaves. Thick, twisted roots anchored it to the ground. That's where the smell of sawdust and scorched bark was coming from.

Annabel was cutting it down.

'She's doing that all wrong,' said Sputnik. 'Anyone can see that if she cuts it at that angle, it's going to fall straight on to the house, smash the roof to bits and kill everyone inside. Why don't folk read the instructions?'

– We've got to stop her!

'You stop her. I don't like to interfere. I'm just a visitor after all.'

I made a grab at the lightsaber, trying to get it off her. Annabel swung it at me, burning the end of my nose. She was unstoppable.

I ran back into the house, flung open the kitchen door. All the parents were standing around chatting. I shouted, 'Quick! The children! Quick!'

They stared at me. Barbara from the caravan site said, 'I thought you said he couldn't talk.'

'Doesn't. Not can't. Of course you can talk, can't you, Prez?'

'The children!'

There was a hideous, creaking, splitting sound from the garden.

Mr Blythe ran out.

The others ran after him.

The tree shook.

It groaned.

There was a snap.

The children were still laughing. That made it even more frightening. Mums and dads grabbed children, dragged them into the house, slammed the door. The tree toppled. Its branches clawed the windows. Its trunk bounced with a hollow thud. Birds screamed. Kids clapped. The littlest one shouted, 'Do it more! Do it more!'

In her mum's arms, Annabel started crying.

'It's all right, sweetheart. You're safe now. Thanks to Prez.'

But I knew she wasn't crying because she had nearly got herself and all her friends crushed in an underage lumberjacking accident. She was crying because she'd dropped the lightsaber and it was buried under the tree. She was crying because she wanted to do more Destruction.

It was amazing the amount of Destruction she had done already. The big farm gate was a row of splinters. The hen house was firewood. The hens were in a state of shock. The tree had fallen so hard one of its branches had stabbed deep into the ground between the cobbles in the farmyard.

'Sputnik?' said Jessie. 'Where's Sputnik?!'

No one said anything. No one needed to. He'd been crushed. Or spiked. Annabel cried louder. Her friends all joined in. Their parents tried to shush them. 'It's all right. You're safe now.'

Then the door banged open. 'Now that,' bawled Sputnik, swaggering in, 'is what you call a party.'

'Sputnik!' cried Jessie, and went and hugged him.

'Thank goodness you're alive!' Sputnik went on, as if it wasn't totally his fault that we were all nearly dead!

'Did you see that tree come down?!' he whooped. '*Wheee!! Crash!* Love it. Nearly wrecked the whole house! This place has THE BEST gravity.'

When I went to bed, Annabel gave me a hug and said, 'Thank you for my happy party, Prez.'

4.
Mooring Hitch Knots

Everyone seemed to think that now I'd finally said something I would start talking. But what could I say?

Sputnik is dangerous?

They thought he was a dog. If you say 'dangerous dog', folk think you're talking about a dog that bites, not someone who hands out deadly weapons at children's parties.

Something had to be done. And I was the one who had to do it. It was like that time that Grandad was the only one awake on his whole ship, and he saw an iceberg floating right at them. The safety of the whole crew was in his hands.

He saved them.

I had to save the Blythes. From Sputnik.

From the top bunk in Ray's room I could see a little light shining in Sputnik's stable.

I sneaked down to the kitchen. The only sound was the hum of the fridge. I slipped out into the yard. If anyone saw me out there in the dark they'd definitely think I was trying to run away. But the curtains were drawn. No one was stirring. In the stables, the ponies were sleeping. The chickens kind of purred as I walked past them, but mostly it was quiet. Really, really quiet. I'd never heard quiet like it.

No traffic.

No voices.

Nothing.

Then something.

A kind of slimy cough.

My heart shrank.

I must have gasped or something, because Sputnik poked his head over the stable door. 'Is that you, Prez? Come in.'

I know now that the slimy noise was a cow coughing. Now if I hear one at night I don't even notice. It's the country version of traffic noise. But I didn't know that then.

Sputnik had really made himself at home in the wee stable. He'd strung up a hammock in the corner using a proper mooring hitch knot. He'd turned the dog basket upside down and made it into a kind of bedside table, with a red notebook on it, a torch and a pencil. 'The reason I asked you to come over—'

– You didn't ask me here! I just came.

'. . . is that I have something very serious to say to you. I think I have to tell Mr and Mrs Blythe that you nearly killed Annabel. And all her friends. On her birthday. You're a danger to this household. Really you should go back to the Temporary.'

– I did what?! It was *you* who nearly killed them!

'You gave her a lightsaber.'

– I gave her a *toy* lightsaber. *You* made it into a real lightsaber.

'It was her birthday! Who would make a child play with a broken toy on her birthday? You need to show more consideration.'

– NO! *You* need to show more consideration. And sense. And—

'We're arguing. That can't be right. The Mellows family always sticks together. Let's agree to never argue again.'

– You armed a five-year-old. She could have decapitated me.

'Actually, lightsabers are rubbish at decapitation.'

– If you get me into trouble, they'll send me

back to the Temporary. And if I go back you can't come with me because they'll think you're a dog and there's no dogs allowed.

'Are you' – tears seemed to fill his big brown eyes – 'throwing me out?'

– No. I'm saying we have to not cause trouble. We have to be good.

'OK. OK. I'll be good if you will. Come on, let's fix the tree.'

– Fix the tree? How do you fix a tree? And don't say read the manual, because trees do not have manuals.

'What made the tree fall down?'

– You did.

'Gravity. Gravity pulled it down so . . . gravity can put it back up.'

– Gravity pulls things *down*. It does not pull things up. Gravity is a one-way street.

Sputnik opened the stable door and strode out into the yard. 'Even the most one-way street ever,' he said, 'has its twists and turns. Ow! That moonlight's a bit strong.' He pulled his goggles down, stuffed his red notebook into his backpack and set off towards the garden.

The moon shone right on the tree trunk, lighting

up the cracks and ripples in its bark. Sputnik climbed on to the trunk and I followed him along it. The tree looked bigger and more wrecked than it had in the daytime. Bark crunched under our feet. Branches creaked. Leaves rattled. A bird that must have been hiding flew up in front of us in a whirr of wings. The moon sailed low overhead. It was like being on a ship. Sputnik stood still, licked his finger and held it in the air, as if he was testing the wind. 'North by north-west,' he said, jumping down off the trunk. 'Couldn't be easier.'

– I can't feel any wind.

'I'm not talking about the wind. I'm talking about the gravity stream. The tree twisted as it fell. All we've got to do is twist it back up again. If we can just get the tree upright . . .'

– How are we going to get a tree upright? I'm a boy, not a crane.

Sputnik sucked his teeth. 'Easy. We'll use the shed!' He put his back to the wall of the shed and started to push. 'Come on. Let's shove it.' The wooden shed stood on a concrete platform. When we shoved it, it scraped across the concrete. The door shook. The window rattled. The latch jingled.

– What are we doing?

'We're trying to launch this shed. Come on.'

– Launch? A shed?

'Gravity's not a sleepy bulldog. It doesn't just plonk itself down on the ground. (Come on, shove harder.) It comes in waves (push it sideways). Way out there, two black holes bump into each other and (nearly there come on) that sends huge gravity waves rolling through the universe (one . . . two . . . three). The waves break on your planet and you've got gravity swishing and swirling everywhere. Very handy if you know how to use it.'

I was expecting the shed to drop off the edge of the concrete on to the grass. It didn't. Very, very slowly, the front end drifted upwards. The back end was still touching the ground. But only touching it – like a balloon. Not really resting on it – like a shed.

'One more little nudge.'

The whole shed wobbled, then straightened up. It was floating in the air.

'There's a gravity eddy just . . . here,' said Sputnik. 'If we can settle the shed on top of it. There we are.'

The shed started to drift away, like one of those paper lanterns with a light inside. When it was a few feet up in the air, Sputnik jumped. No, he didn't jump, he leaped. He bent his knees and sprang, catapulting himself in through the door of the shed. He reached into his backpack and tugged out a bright blue rope. 'Grab the rope!' he called, dangling one end in front of me. 'Get the tree! Great. Great job. Now, hold on.' I had slung the rope around the biggest branch. 'Can you tie it on?'

Of course I could. Grandad was always very clear about the importance of being able to tie a good firm knot. I could do a clove hitch, a half hitch, a reef, a stopper, a . . .

'Just tie the knot!'

I tied a proper bowline knot, grabbed a handful of the lag and we both pulled it tight. Next thing I knew, I was leaning in through the shed doorway with my legs dangling behind. Sputnik pulled me in. 'Welcome aboard!' he said. 'Climb right in. We need the weight.'

– Won't the shed stop floating if it weighs more?

'You really don't understand a thing about gravity, do you? The more mass a thing has, the more gravity it has. The more gravity the shed has, the more easily it'll lift the tree.'

We leaned out of the door. The shed floated higher and higher until the rope grew taut. It tugged at the tree.

'Jump up and down! That usually helps.'

We bounced around inside the shed for a while, making it rock from side to side. Soon it leaned sideways as though it was taking a breath, then shot upwards so fast that we sat down, giggling, in surprise. Through the doorway we could see the huge tree rising like a giant waking up. Its branches clutched at the air as it steadied itself.

'Haul her in,' ordered Sputnik. 'Bring her round.'

We hauled on the rope. The tree turned, its arms stretched out, like those of a massive dancer. It waved once and stopped still. The fallen trunk had clicked back into place on the stump.

'There. I knew this place had the best gravity. You may be a danger to life and limb, but you know how to fix a tree.'

I'd tied the rope around one of the biggest branches, about halfway up the tree. Now that the tree was standing upright, the shed floated right up as far as the rope would allow. We sat in the doorway, looking down on the treetop.

'Look what I found in the branches,' said Sputnik.

It was the red lightsaber.

I didn't want anything more to do with lightsabers. I just wanted to sit and look out across the farm and the hill. Quick little shadows fluttered all around us.

'Bats,' said Sputnik. 'Going back to their home in the tree.' Everything went hush. Sounds we didn't know we were listening to stopped. As if someone had pushed the world's mute button. A feathery shape ghosted by.

'Barn owl,' said Sputnik. 'Did you hear how everything went quiet? Even you stopped breathing for a second. No one wants to be eaten by the owl. Oh. Hear that?'

I couldn't hear anything.

'A bat's last squeak. The owl just swallowed it whole.'

The moon was higher in the sky now and smaller. But the stars . . . the stars were fierce bright and there were billions and billions of them, like grains of sugar spilled on a huge blackboard. I know now that the sky looks like that every night if you go somewhere dark enough. But that was the first time I'd ever seen the night sky properly. The shed rocked like a ship at anchor in a sea of stars. Sputnik took off his goggles and sniffed. 'Woodsmoke, roses, wild garlic, lemonade, beer. Lovely peaceful smells. Want a cigar?'

He took a cigar the size of a hot dog out of his pocket, snipped off the end with his scissors, then lit it with the lightsaber.

– Smoking is so bad for you. Why does everyone think you're a dog?

'I'm just very – you know – adaptable.'

– But you don't look like a dog to me. Why not?

'Because you are the reason I'm here.'

5.
Laika

'A long time ago,' said Sputnik, 'we came across a tiny primitive spacecraft – Sputnik II – the very one that was flown by Laika.'

– Who?

'Laika. You must have heard of her. I thought everyone on your planet would have heard of her. Laika the dog. First Earth creature in space.'

– No.

'Well the R-7 sustainer on her craft was packing in. She was just drifting around space, running out of oxygen, so we rescued her and took her in.'

– Wait a minute. Why did you call it *my* planet? Where are you from? Space?

'Everyone is from space. There's nowhere else to be from. What do you think this planet is floating around in? Soup? Listen. So we rescued Laika and she told us all about this planet. But the things she said about it sounded too good to be true. She made it sound like a magical, mythical place. So no one believed her. And she looked so sad that I decided to defend her. I said, 'Just because a place is magical and mythical, does that mean it's not real?'

'And everyone said, "Well, yes, it does, to be honest." Then I said, "Lo! I am Sputnik, and Sputnik says nothing in this universe is too good to be true." Then I took an oath. I said, "I will voyage to the ends of the universe in search of the magical, mythical Earth and if I find it, I'll let you know. Goodbye."

'And now I've found it. I went off and discovered your planet. Thanks to me, your planet is now a real planet. Not a fairy tale. What do you think? How does it feel? More solid? More wet? More gritty?'

– No. It was always pretty solid. And wet.

'Before I left, Laika gave me a copy of the guidebook to Earth she'd written.'

He pulled a little red school notebook out of his bag. On the title page someone had written 'Laika's Companion to Life on Earth'.

I flicked through it.

'It was written with this special pen,' said Sputnik, 'that can write in weightless conditions and never runs out of ink.'

– We have those. We call them pencils.

'Yeah. Amazing piece of technology. What do you think of the book? Is it accurate?'

The book was a list of all the good things about Earth.

It said, on Earth everything is edible.

– That's not true for a start.

It said that on Earth there is a race called humans . . .

– That's true. That's me. I'm a human.

. . . and another race called dogs.

– Laika was a dog.

If you're visiting Earth, you should definitely go as a dog. Dogs are the dominant species.

– Hmmm. Not sure about that.

Humans will bring you food, throw balls for you to fetch. When you do a poo they pick it up and put it in a bin for you. They welcome you into their home.

– Those things are probably mostly true.

'So this book, it's not accurate?'

– Maybe that's how Earth looks if you're a dog, but it's not the whole story.

'OK,' said Sputnik. He flipped his pencil over and started to rub out everything in the book. 'More amazing technology,' he said. 'It allows you to move on from your mistakes.'

In the end there were just a few sentences left on one page. 'I nearly forgot about this,' he said. 'It says, "Please say hello to Mellows of Traquair Gardens, Dumfries." That's you, isn't it?'

– Yes, but how would she know about me?

'"And please take care of him, signed Laika." Now I've passed the message on, I can rub that out too.'

– I don't understand how she could possibly know about me.

'You're both from the same planet, aren't you?'

– But it's a big planet.

– 'It might look big to you. In terms of the universe, if you're from the same planet, that's local. That's more or less next door. In terms of the

56

universe, she might as well have been sitting on your knee. Oh, and she sent you a present. She said it would make you smile.'

He fished out of his backpack something that looked like an old red rubber ball. It had a rash of toothmarks and it was coming undone across the seam. I didn't really want to touch it in case of germs.

– Why would an old rubber ball make me smile?

'I don't know. To be honest I was expecting you to be a dog. She said you were her friend and I thought any friend of Laika's is probably a dog. That's why I morphed into dog form.'

– So you don't normally look like a dog? What do you normally look like?

'I normally look like me. Anyway, I promised to look after you.'

– Look after me? Why would I need anyone to look after me? I've been looking after myself for years. I've been looking after Grandad too.

'You need me to look after you because you're in incredible danger. I'm here to save you.'

– What kind of danger?

'Didn't I mention? Earth is about to be destroyed.'

6.
The Companion

'Now that I have proved that Earth *does* exist,' said Sputnik, 'I have to prove that it *should* exist. Every planet has to have a reason.'

– Isn't a planet just a planet?

'Look up at the stars.'

I looked again at the caster-sugar stars. If anything, there seemed to be more of them. The whole sky shimmered with them.

'Space is crowded. Nebulae are pumping out new stars by the dozen, day in, day out. Someone has to make room for them. That someone is Planetary Clearance. They get rid of all the useless old stars and planets to make room for new celestial bodies. It's called pan-galactic decluttering. So as soon as I told them I'd found the magical, mythical planet Earth, they said, "OK, we'll be right over to shrink it."'

– WHAT?! You can't shrink a planet.

My only experience of things shrinking was once when I put Grandad's jumper in the washing machine on the wrong setting and it came out looking like a jumper for a toy.

'Useless planets are being shrunk all over the sky. Their sun shrinks to the size of a planet – it's called a white dwarf; look it up – and its planets shrink to the size of golf balls.'

– But this planet isn't useless. It's really useful.

'That's what I said. And they said, "Planet Earth has been mythical for years. How can a place be any use if it's mythical?"'

– But it's not mythical! You proved it.

'Exactly. If a planet is worth keeping, it's worth seeing. That's why Laika wrote her guidebook. But now we've rubbed out everything that was in it, it's empty. That means Earth isn't worth seeing.'

– But we must be able to do something?!

'We could write a new *Companion to Earth*. It's just a list. You just have to find ten things worth seeing or doing, I'll write them in the notebook and then Earth can carry on waltzing around its little sun. I'm sure you could write a great guidebook.'

– To here? I don't know anything about here.

I've only been here a few days.

'Not to Stramoddie, you fool. To Earth. How much do you know about Earth?'

– Well, I've lived on it all my life. Plus when Grandad first started taking care of me I was still a wean. So he had to take me with him on his voyages across the Seven Seas. Remember the map? In with my stuff? That's all the places I've been.

Sputnik whistled. 'That's a lot of places. The Amazon, Shangri-La . . . You've been everywhere. What was Shangri-La like?'

– Well, I was pretty young . . . I can't remember

the details. I don't think it can be very nice though. Grandad used to say, 'I hope I don't end up in Shangri-La.'

'You see? We've already got something *not* to put on the list and nothing *to* put on the list. We're minus one before we've even started. This is a very disappointing planet. Nearly everything that Laika said was wrong.'

– I can make a list. I'm sure I can. I'm good at making lists.

'You're sure? You've got all the time in the world, but there isn't as much time in the world as you think.'

– How long have we got?

'See that bunch of stars there, like a kite? When they reach the top of the sky, Planetary Clearance move in and Earth becomes a pocket planet.'

– This is the first time I've really seen stars. How fast do they move? Are they going to get there in ten minutes or ten years?

'You've got the rest of the summer. If we haven't finished *Sputnik's Guide to Life on Earth* by then, that's it. What's the first thing?'

– How about this? What we're looking at now? The stars and the moon and—

'No. For one thing, stars are not on Earth.

– No. But you can steer a ship around the world with them. Grandad taught me. See that V-shaped constellation there? That's . . .

'They're also not amazing.'

– What?!?

'Stars are the most unamazing things in existence. The entire universe is crawling with stars and planets and comets and nebulae. Wherever you go, there's no getting away from them. They're everywhere. They're usual. I'm looking for something *un*usual.'

– So I have to find ten things that are more amazing than stars?

'Yes. Think you can do it?'

– Not really.

'Go on! You are ideally qualified for the job. Plus you're the only person I've met who I can communicate with.'

– I don't talk.

'Exactly. You listen. Which is so much better. I talk all the time, but no one listens. You never say a word, so everyone listens . . .'

It was true. Sometimes if I just coughed or sneezed, everyone turned to look at me.

'So?'

– I have to try. I don't want anyone shrinking my planet.

'So I'll take care of you. And you take care of the planet.'

– I don't need taking care of. You just concentrate on you. Just one thing.

'What?'

– I don't want to have to leave the planet. Actually I don't even want to leave Stramoddie. Not yet. I'm just the kid from the Temporary. If there's trouble, they'll send me back there. And you are trouble.

'OK. I'll try to be good.'

– They think you're a dog, remember.

'So I'll be a good dog. How hard can that be? If a dog can be good, I can too. What makes a good dog?'

– I don't know. I've never had a dog. I guess a dog that doesn't bark. Maybe it helps around the farm. A working dog.

'So I should milk the cows? Drive the quad bike? Make some phone calls?'

– No, dogs don't do any of those things. Just be friendly. And cute. Sometimes you see a dog go and fetch the paper from the shop. That's good.'

'So we're back to fetching now,' said Sputnik. 'I told you I don't do fetching.'

– You did ask.

That's when it struck me. He was asking me to save the Earth. I can't save the Earth. I couldn't even save my own grandad. I'm just a kid from the Temporary.

– Wait! Wait. Earth is going to be destroyed and you didn't even mention it! How am I going to sleep if my planet might be destroyed? Shouldn't we be out there right now looking for things worth saving?

'You need to pace yourself. You've got weeks to save the Earth. Get some sleep.'

– How can I sleep if I'm facing Doom for All Mankind?

'Turn around three times before you lie down. Works every time. If you turn round fast enough, your worries can't keep up. When your head hits the pillow, it's empty.'

– That's what dogs do.

'We can learn a lot from observing other species.'

So I tried it. I turned around three times and snuggled down.

Turning around three times might have worked for Sputnik, but it didn't work for me.

I spent the whole night thinking about how I was

going to save the world. How was I going to impress someone who could levitate a tree? Someone who's seen a star die. Travelled across space. The more I thought about it, the more everything on Earth seemed little and ordinary.

I tried Googling the Wonders of the World, but all the best ones were ruined or lost.

When the sun came up I got to thinking, Maybe he was just winding me up. No one can *really* shrink a planet, can they? So I Googled 'white dwarfs' and it turns out that, yes, suns and planets are shrinking all the time.

I really wished Grandad was here to help. Grandad had been everywhere, seen everything, knew everything. Every night after tea we used to sit on the couch in front of the telly and shout at the news. And *The One Show*. And *Match of the Day*. And the adverts. He knew more about politics than the politicians did, more about football than the footballers. He even shouted at some of the fridge magnets, especially the one of the Leaning Tower of Pisa. 'I could put that tower straight easy,' he used to say. 'It's all about the underpinning!'

He also knew everything about cooking. It was Grandad who showed me how to chop vegetables really fast. Maybe that would impress Sputnik. Maybe I could make him a big paella, the way Grandad showed me. I bet they didn't have paella where Sputnik came from.

Or fish stew. Grandad made amazing fish stew. Or he did before he started forgetting things. Such as when he forgot to turn the cooker on and tried to make us eat the fish stew raw. Or when he forgot people's names and tried to hide it by calling everyone 'bud', including my form teacher. Or when he forgot that it's OK to shout at your own telly, but not to shout at other people's. He shouted at the one in the post-office queue, which was showing a film about how to claim your pension. He shouted at the ones in the window of Wilson's Electrical on George Street.

It was just after that that they took him away. The man from the Children's Temporary Accommodation said, 'I'm afraid your grandad can no longer look after you at the present time.'

I was going to say, 'He doesn't look after me. We look after each other,' but I didn't. I asked if he was going to get better soon. He said, 'We can but hope.'

I thought I spent all night worrying about these things. I couldn't imagine having a nap when you were supposed to be trying to save the Earth. But I must have fallen asleep in the end because I remember being woken up by the wind blowing through the broken window.

I looked around the shed.

Sputnik had vanished.

7.
1kg Plain Flour, 1 Tub Margarine, 500g Mushrooms

I checked that we were back on the ground before opening the shed door. The air was fresh and cool, which made me realize I really needed the toilet.

– Come on, Sputnik, let's go in.

No sign of him in the yard.

Or on the lane.

Or in the field.

He was gone.

Maybe he was upset that I had told him off for introducing deadly weapons to the birthday party.

The tree was standing tall. In fact it looked as though it had always been there. Maybe the tree falling down had been a dream.

Surely the floating shed was a dream.

As if a gravity eddy could ever be a thing.

Maybe I didn't need to save the world after all!

I opened the kitchen door.

'There he is!!
He's here,
everyone!
Look!
Phew!'

'Prez!
You SCARED us.
We thought
you'd run off.'

'She thought
you'd run
away with
Sputnik.'

'Where were you?'

'Your bed
wasn't slept in.'

'He slept in the shed.
I saw him come out.
    He slept in the shed with Sputnik.'

'Well, you're here now.
Thank the Lord.'

'But please don't sleep in the shed again.
    If word got out that you were
    sleeping in the shed, they'd come
    and take you away as soon as . . .'

'Look!
  Look. At. That.'   'What?'

'Where's Sputnik?'

'The tree!
The tree is back up!'

'I called the forestry last night.
I never expected them to get it done so quickly.'

'I don't get it.
The tree fell down.
How can it be up?'

'That's amazing.
I didn't hear a thing. Did you?'

'Where's Sputnik?'

'But how can the tree be
up if it was down?'

'It was uprooted and I suppose
they just re-rooted it?'

'Has anyone
seen Sputnik?'

'How can a tree . . . ?'

'He isn't in the shed.'

'Who isn't?'

'Sputnik. He's run off.'

'Oh. Now this is serious.
This is bad. This is very bad.'

The dad walked up and down and bit his lip and talked for a long time about how bad bad bad it was that a strange dog was loose somewhere on the farm.

'I brought the cows in for milking this morning,' said the mum. 'They didn't seem unusually agitated. And the chickens are fine.'

'Actually the big red one is missing,' said Ray.

'That's because I killed it,' said the mum. 'For Sunday dinner.'

'Ah.'

'So he's not bothering any of our animals.'

'That's good,' said the dad, but then added, 'No, that's bad. If he's not bothering *our* animals, maybe he's bothering someone else's. Maybe he's worrying Dougie's sheep? Or maybe he's down at the caravan site. He could be creating all kinds of havoc down there.'

I wanted to tell them that they didn't have to worry about things like that with Sputnik. But how could I say, 'Calm down. He's not a dog. He's a wee alien in a kilt and goggles'?

The mum was at the computer. 'First thing we do,' she said, 'is Facebook everyone to keep an eye out for him. Put him on the Farms Forum too. Now, has anyone got a photo we can post?'

They all went through the photos on their phones. They had pictures of the party, the cake, the fallen tree. But no one had a picture of Sputnik.

'I know I took pictures of him.
                        That's weird.'

'Never mind.
We can just describe him.
What would you say?
Black-and-white mongrel, mostly collie
dog, pleasant temperament . . .'

'Collie?
He's more of a
Labrador, surely.'

'I thought he was
mostly spaniel.
He looks like a spaniel.'

'What are you talking about?
Spaniels are tiny. Sputnik's a big dog.
Like a lurcher cross.'

'Yeah, he's at least
three-quarters
Alsatian.'

'What do you mean, black
and white? He's brown.'

'I can't see Alsatian in him. He's more of
a retriever or springer type of thing, with
that lovely golden coat of his.'

'Alsatian.'

'Labrador.'

'Lurcher.'

So . . . when I looked at Sputnik, I saw a wee lad in flying goggles and a kilt with a yellow backpack.

And when the Blythes looked at Sputnik they saw a dog.

But every Blythe saw a different kind of dog!

How can you organize a search for someone you can't describe?

They were all still shouting the names of breeds of dog at each other when I heard the doorbell go, just like it did on the night he arrived.

'Is that the doorbell?' said Ray.

'We don't have a doorbell,' said the mum.

'Oh yeah.'

They all carried on talking over each other.

I answered the door. I knew who it was. There's only one person on Earth who carries his own doorbell round with him.

Sputnik went straight past me, carrying a shopping bag. 'Did you miss me?'

– I was worried about you.

'I left a message for you outside the shed. Didn't you tell them?'

– I didn't see a message.

'You don't see messages. You smell them.'

– Oh.

Then I realized what he was talking about. When dogs pee on lamp posts and gateposts, that's their way of communicating. Other dogs come along and sniff the wee and they know whose territory it is or whatever.

'Exactly. I was told the most popular form of communication on the planet was urine.'

– For dogs. Not people.

'So you didn't get the message?'

– No. I don't speak pee. I was worried that you'd run away because the planet was going to be destroyed.

'This planet is not going to be destroyed. Sputnik and Prez are unbeatable. We will save this planet. Probably. Possibly. Look! You told me to be good. And I've been good. The Sputnik is a creature as

74

good as his word. I fixed the tree and now I've done this. They're going to love it.'

He swung into the kitchen, waltzed up to the mum and handed her a newspaper.

'Oh! You brought me a newspaper. I thought dogs only did that in cartoons. What a clever, clever dog you are.' She scratched him behind the ear. 'He must have gone all the way down to Dmitri's shop on the caravan site.'

Sputnik winked at me.

'That *is* clever,' said the dad. 'I'm still not happy about him just wandering off though. You two were supposed to be responsible.' He gave me and Jessie a hard stare.

Then Sputnik plonked his shopping bag down in front of him. The dad looked inside. 'What's here?' he said. 'Oh. A bag of plain flour, a tub of margarine, mushrooms . . . This is everything that was on my shopping list.' He looked at the fridge door, where the shopping list should have been. It wasn't there; it was stuck to the top of the margarine tub. 'Right,' said the dad, 'I'll cook a chicken-and-mushroom pie then. Nice work, Sputnik.'

'Come on,' said Ray. 'Sputnik couldn't have done that. One of you two did it really. You're playing a trick on us. You took him to the shop and did the shopping.'

'Not me,' said Jessie. 'I thought he was missing.'

'Prez then?' said Ray.

I didn't even know there *was* a shop on the caravan site. I didn't even know the way to the caravan site.

'Just a very, very clever dog,' said the mum.

'With a bank account?' said Ray. Everyone looked at him. 'Or how did he pay for it all?'

'That's a wee puzzle,' said the mum. 'Which I'm sure Prez will solve for us when he's ready. Meanwhile I'm sure we're all glad that Sputnik is making himself useful.'

'No problem.' Sputnik smiled. He shook hands with everyone again. Whenever he shook hands with them they all forgot to be worried or puzzled about anything. They just loved those handshakes.

But when he came to shake my hand, I thought . . .

– How *did* you pay for it?

He just winked.

8.
Milk

I didn't want to think about how Sputnik might have got those groceries. I just thought, The sooner I save this planet the better. I didn't have Grandad to help me, but I did have his map. He'd drawn it himself in blue ink, and written all the place names in lovely slanty handwriting, then drawn a fancy compass in the top right-hand corner, an inaccurate dolphin in the bottom left and a scroll, with 'The Travels of Prez and His Grandad' written on it, unfurling across the top. Then he'd rolled it up and tied it with ribbon. It really was like a proper pirate map. When I unrolled it, it smelt of our flat in Traquair Gardens. I looked at all the places I'd seen and somehow forgotten. Shangri-La. Pisa. Murmansk. I Googled them on Ray's computer. It made me feel better. They were all amazing. In Murmansk there were giant ships with factory-sized icebergs floating past them. Huge walruses lolled around, their tusks as big as me. Up the Amazon, giant snakes hung from the branches of the trees. The white domes of lost cities rose out of jungles.

I decided to make a list.

1. The Amazon.
2. The Great Pyramid, Egypt.
3. A different great pyramid, Mexico.
4. The Taj Mahal, India.
5. Murmansk, Russia.
6. Shangri-La . . .

I didn't notice Ray looking over my shoulder until he said, 'The Amazon? You've been up the Amazon?'

According to the map I had.

'And Shangri-La? Really?! I thought Shangri-La was a made-up place. I thought it was a mythical kingdom in the Himalayas.'

— Well, that explained why Grandad didn't want to end up there. Who would want to end up somewhere mythical?

'The Taj Mahal?! You've seen the Taj Mahal?! Dairy farmers never go anywhere. If we went to the Taj Mahal, we'd have to take the cows with us. Every summer everyone else in my class goes off to Spain or Florida or Blackpool or whatever. And we're stuck here at Stramoddie making hay. You know what our holiday is, Prez? When the Temporary Kid comes to stay with us. *You* are the holiday. Be a good holiday, eh? Bring me sunshine.' He stepped into his boots and headed outside.

I hadn't thought about the fact that there had been other Temporary Kids before me. I wondered who they were. Did they all get the top bunk? Were some of them more fun than me?

From the bedroom window I could see Ray starting to help his dad fix the fence where the tree had crashed into it. The dad was driving a thing like a miniature digger. Ray was piling the bits into the scoop. I was about to go down and make myself useful when Sputnik bounced in.

'Ready to save your little world?!'

– You're not allowed indoors except the kitchen.

'Then let's go! Is this the Ten Things Worth Seeing? What's that? Is it far?'

'It's the world's most beautiful building.'

'Stop right there. Buildings don't count.'

– What?!

'Buildings are nothing but architecture. I'm not

interested in architecture. Not human architecture anyway. Humans can't build for toffee.'

– Oh.

Panic exploded in my brain like popcorn. What was I supposed to do now? Nearly all the Wonders of the World are human architecture.

– What other kinds of architecture are there?

'Bee architecture. Have you ever been inside a bee hive? Now *that* is architecture. Hexagonal combs running with honey. Light. And the sound! Hundreds of bees working away. Prawns and the like, they build too. Coral reefs. They built them out of their own bodies. So. The Taj Mahal . . . I don't like the sound of it.'

– What *do* you like the sound of? This is serious. I'm trying to save a planet here.

He clutched his ears and yowled. 'Well, I don't like the sound of *that* for a start! Make it stop!' as if he was in pain. For a second I thought the world was ending there and then.

– What's happening? Are you OK? What's wrong?

'Can't you hear that? It's like someone's drilling in my eardrums.'

– What is it?

'A whistle. Can't you hear? It must be around 53 kilohertz!'

I looked out of the window. Jessie was in the yard, holding a dog leash and blowing into a little silver whistle.

– It's Jessie. I think she's got a dog whistle.

'I'll soon put a stop to that.' Sputnik opened his backpack. The room was suddenly filled with a hot, fireworky smell. He pulled out a pistol. A *real* pistol. It looked like something from *Pirates of the Caribbean*; heavy, with a big brass hammer at the back, a silver trigger and a wooden handle.

– Whoa. Stop.

'I'll shoot over her head. Just to frighten her.'

– Oh no no no. Oh. Wait. Oh no. Oh.

– My.

– Days.

– That's how you got the shopping this morning, isn't it?! You pulled a gun in Dmitri's shop!

'Guns are so useful. When you want stuff without paying for it.'

He was at the window. He was aiming at Jessie.

– No. No. Stop. Definitely stop.

'She's the one who needs to stop.'

– Then we'll go down and stop her with good manners. NOT WITH GUNS.

Even when we got right up to Jessie I still couldn't hear the whistle, just a faint thumping sound. When she saw us coming she took it out of her mouth.

Sputnik said, 'Thank the stars for that.' Then the thumping stopped and I realized it hadn't been the whistle at all. It was my heart worrying about him pulling a gun.

Ray came over to look at the whistle. 'We got that in the feed store, remember? We used to use it in that game . . .'

'Dogs of the Future. I loved that game.'

'Don't talk about it in front of the Temporary Kid. It's embarrassing.'

'And don't talk about the Temporary Kid in front of the Temporary Kid. Maybe he doesn't talk, but he does have ears. Hi, Prez!'

'Hi, Prez,' Jessie smiled. Then she dived on Sputnik and fixed an old-looking collar round his neck. The leather was all cracked and it had a little brass medal attached that had been worn smooth. 'What do you think?'

'Love it,' said Sputnik. 'Is it a local custom? I love local customs.'

– It's a local custom if you're a dog. You're not a dog.

'Who cares about the species? It's the thought that counts.'

But while he was talking Jessie had clipped a leash to the collar and now she started dragging him down the lane towards the cow pasture. Sputnik was disgusted.

'What's she doing?! Ow! She's dragging me. Does she think I'm her luggage?'

'Come on, Sputnik,' trilled Jessie. 'Walkies.'

'Walkies? Are you nuts? We've got a planet to save! Tell her.'

– How can I tell her? What would I say? 'Your dog is not a dog, and by the way an extra-terrestrial demolition gang is going to come and knock your planet down very soon so could you unclip the leash, please?'

'That about sums it up. OW! She keeps pulling.'

– If I said that, they'd have me back to the Temporary. Only it wouldn't be temporary any more.

'Sit, Sputnik! Sit!' said Jessie, pointing at the ground.

'I'll sit when you bring me a chair,' said Sputnik. 'I'm not sitting here. It's covered in mud.'

'Sit!'

– Yes, I'll sit. When we find something hygienic to sit on.

They call the long lane running down to the farm 'the loaning'. Sputnik trotted off down it. Some of the cows looked up as he passed. Sputnik stopped. He stared.

'What are they?'

– Cows.

'Cows,' said Sputnik, rolling the word around his mouth like a new flavour.

'Stay,' said Jessie, crouching down in front of him. 'Sputnik, stay.' She held a finger up in his face. 'Stay, stay, stay . . .'

'I think you've made yourself fairly clear,' said Sputnik. 'You want me to stay here, is that right?'

'Good boy.' Very slowly she undid the leash and walked away from him backwards. 'Good boy. Good Sputnik.'

'So. Cows,' Sputnik hissed out of the corner of his mouth. 'Are they . . . edible?'

– No.

'They *smell* edible.'

– Well, you *can* eat them, but first you have to . . .

'Great! I'm STAAARRVING!' He didn't wait for me to finish. He was just gone.

'SPUTNIK!' yelled Jessie. 'Come here, boy! Come here, Sputnik.'

But Sputnik wasn't coming here. Sputnik hurled himself over the fence, straight into the middle of the herd of cows. What was he going to do? Bite a cow?!

The cows didn't wait to find out.

They mooed.

They rolled their eyes.

They fled in one big bumping mud-flinging ground-banging cow-riot.

'Sputnik! NOOO!!!' howled Jessie.

I went after him. Cows thundered over the pasture in the direction of the hill behind the house. I ran after them. What was I planning to do? Grab them by their tails or something?

The dad came striding over the hill towards us in his wellies. 'Whoa there! Whoa! What's going on?!' He waved a big stick. 'What's Sputnik doing in the field?' The cows were going round in circles now. 'Look at the cows! This is a stampede! They're bouncing around so much their milk will be yogurt by the time we get it in the can. You have to control him, Prez. You have to be responsible.'

'No one,' snarled Sputnik, pushing his mud-spattered goggles up on to the top of his head and looking the dad in the eye, 'controls Sputnik.'

'It's my fault!' called Jessie, running up the field. 'I'm sorry. I'm sorry.'

'I was bringing them in for milking. It's going to take ages to settle them now.'

'It was my fault,' said Jessie again. 'I won't do it again. Don't send him away.'

I wasn't sure if she was talking about Sputnik or me.

'Fuss about nothing,' said Sputnik. 'You just have to be assertive. He probably heard something like *Arrff Arrff Woof*.'

Obviously the dad didn't hear that. He said, 'Take Sputnik back into the house before he does any more damage.'

But Sputnik stood with his hands on his hips on the top of the rise and shouted, 'Lady mammals! Look at me. Come on, look at me.' The cows turned their big wet eyes towards him. 'Am I going to eat you? YES, I AM!' The cows made a cow-fuss. 'UNLESS – are you listening? – UNLESS you do as you're told. If you do as you're told I won't eat you. Even though you smell tasty.'

'At least keep him quiet,' said the dad.

'Lady mammals!' bawled Sputnik. 'Form an orderly queue. Go and get yourselves milked. You know you want to really.'

The cows stopped mooing.

They also stopped panicking, running, barging and pooing.

They formed an orderly queue.

'Oh,' said the dad. The cows walked, one behind the other, up the hill, as though they were queuing for their pensions in the post office.

'Right,' shrugged the dad, scratching his head as the cows filed by. 'Well. Things seem to have settled down a bit. So. Keep Sputnik under control and you can come and help with the milking.'

I followed the dad and Jessie and the cows over the hill. At the top, I stopped and stared.

'Good, eh?' said the dad.

In the dip at the bottom of the hill was a castle. It was very small for a castle. But it was definitely a castle. It had a tower and tall windows and a moat and a drawbridge even.

'Some people have a milking parlour,' said the dad. 'We have a milking castle. It's famous.'

'Everyone calls it the Coo Palace,' said Jessie, 'My great-grandad built it. The roof leaks and the tower's a wee bit wonky . . .'

'That's just the underpinning,' said Sputnik. 'I could easily fix that.'

– Like the Leaning Tower of Pisa. That's been wonky for hundreds of years and it still hasn't fallen down.

'You've seen the Leaning Tower of Pisa?' said Sputnik.

– Course. One of the things I saw when I was travelling.

'What's it like?'

– Well it was quite . . . leany.

'Leany?'

– I don't remember that much. I was really young. Leaning. It was leaning.

Jessie didn't hear that obviously; she just kept talking. She really loved that Coo Palace. 'I love it. I bet the cows love it too. It's like Cow Hogwarts! I bet our cows boast about it to other cows. It's got a real drawbridge. Come and see.'

We ran ahead and she showed me how to work the handle so that the drawbridge came down. The cows strolled over it and into a kind of courtyard. 'Once they're all in, we have to pull the drawbridge up again. Then they're in this holding area, see? Now we slide back these big doors. Not too fast. And we count the first fifteen cows into the milking parlour. Then close it again quick. You have to shoo any cow that's trying to follow the others. Now we go in the wee door. We'll have to leave Sputnik out here. Inside it's a clean area. Come on. I'll show you how to wash the udders. You can make yourself useful.'

I really did want to make myself useful. I just never

thought that would mean wiping cows' underneath bits with a cloth dipped in iodine.

'Cleans the udder,' said the dad. 'Also tells the cow to get ready for milking.'

After that we went round attaching the pumps to the udders. Jessie showed me how. It felt a bit weird but the cows didn't seem to mind, and it was easy once you got the hang of it. Then the dad threw a switch and a deep sloshing sound ran all around us through the pipes. The dad put his hand on my shoulder and Jessie said, 'Hear that? That's the milk that we milked.'

I *could* hear that. I could hear a different sound too. A strange, windy moaning.

'We really should sort that roof out,' said the dad. 'Listen to the wind wailing up there. Horrible sound.'

But I knew it wasn't the wind. I'd heard that sound before. It was Sputnik blowing into Grandad's harmonica. I wondered how he'd got hold of it.

Even though he was making such a stramash and was standing miles away from me, he still heard my wondering.

'I stole it!' he yelled. 'Your grandad won't mind. This is a musical instrument. It wants to be played, not hidden away in a backpack.'

– You're not playing it. You're just blowing into it.

'Sounds beautiful to me.'

– It sounds like something dying inside a washing machine to me.

He took a deep breath. 'Hmmm,' he said, 'Cow dung, cow wee, cow's breath, cow's milk and just a hint of salt and seaweed. I must admit I'm surprised to discover that cows are electric. What are you doing? Recharging them?'

– They're not electric. The pumps are. The pumps are for getting the milk out.

'Cows have milk in?! Cows are meat with milk in the middle? No wonder they live in a palace. They're amazing! Are you sure I couldn't eat just one?'

– Where are you? I can hear you but I can't see you.

'Can you hear Sputnik?' said Jessie.

'Is he in here somewhere?' asked the dad.

'Up here!' yelled Sputnik.

I looked up. The others followed my gaze. We were standing right under the tower. You could see a square of sky where it was open at the top. You could also see Sputnik looking down at us, goggles flashing.

'How did he get up there?' said Jessie. 'The stairs are in here.'

He probably rode an anti-gravity cow up to the top.

'If I fiddled with the temperature of these pipes,' said Sputnik, 'I could make ice cream come out of the cows instead of milk.'

– Don't.

'But imagine – a big cow filled with ice cream. Come on. Who wouldn't want a bite of that?'

'Hold on, Sputnik!' called the dad, who seemed to think Sputnik didn't want to be at the top of the tower. 'We're coming to get you.'

Climbing the stairs to the top of the tower was like climbing up a corkscrew of cobwebs. I scraped my arm twice. I felt a bit dizzy by the time I got to the top, but then the fresh air hit me, and so did the view. Fields dipped and rolled all the way up and down the valley. You couldn't see the farmhouse because it was snuggled in a fold of the hill, but you could see the smoke from its chimney wandering off into the sky. There was a line of trees cresting the hill like a fancy haircut. There was something that looked like a lot of Lego, which turned out to be the caravan site. In the opposite direction, the ground seemed to be shining.

'Is that the sea?' asked Sputnik. 'Haven't seen a sea in thousands of light years. Last sea I saw was the Sea of Peril.'

– Where's that? I've never heard of it.

'The far end of the Pup solar system. As seas go, it's disappointing. No gravity. No tide. Also no water.'

– How can you have a sea without water?

'By having a sea of poisonous gas.'

– Ah.

'According to the stories, there are seas all over this planet. Seven of them in fact. What's this one called?'

'This is Rumblecairn Bay and that's the Merse,' said the dad, as though he had understood what Sputnik was saying. 'It's the bit where the sea goes when the tide comes in. Some people like a nice sandy beach, but we prefer the Merse, don't we, Jess?'

'The what?' said Sputnik.

The dad stared at him. 'You know,' he said, 'sometimes I could swear he understands everything I'm saying.'

The Merse is basically a lot of mud, but Jessie seemed happy to talk about it until the tide came in: 'I love the way it shines when the sun comes up.

Sand doesn't do that. And if you know where to look there's all kinds of things. Crabs and mussels and natterjacks. There's a creek. And there's a stretch where if you don't look where you're stepping, you can wind up in mud up to your middle; that happened to me once. That line of big wooden poles – that's for the salmon nets. See? I always thought if I ever got caught with the tide coming in, I could hold on to one of them and pretend I was a salmon that's been caught. They're covered in mussels and wee limpets so sharp you could cut rope on them. There's a little stone jetty down that way because this used to be a port – for moving cows and for stone from the quarry. Then there are the wader birds – the redshanks and the curlews – they walk like they're on stilts. "Merse" is a Viking word, you know. Everyone thinks the Vikings were mad boys, but they weren't really, were they, Dad? They just didn't have enough land. When a bairn grew to be a man, his dad would send him out to find a wee bit of land for himself. Then when *he* had bairns, he'd do the same. That's why they spread out all over the world. They were just looking for a home, you know? They brought these cows with them. Not these exact cows. But their ancestors. They're called

Belties. See the way the white band goes right round the middle. Belty, see?

'And that hill there with the trees on top. That's a Roman fort. From the days of Hadrian's Wall.'

'Hadrian's what?' said Sputnik.

'Hadrian's Wall,' said the dad. Again it was almost like he could understand every word Sputnik was saying. Maybe because he was a cow farmer he was used to talking to other species. 'The Romans built it. Hadrian was a Roman emperor. Well, he was emperor of Rome. He actually came from Spain. So did most of the soldiers on the wall.'

Grandad was born in Spain. He went all over the world with the navy, then he met my gran and ended up in Scotland. Just like a Viking. Or a soldier in the Roman army.

'Hadrian built the wall to keep the Scots out of England. As if we'd ever want to leave a place as bonnie as this.'

'A wall?' said Sputnik. 'How big was this wall?'

– It's eighty-four miles long. It goes from Bowness to Newcastle. One side of the country to the other.

I was surprised by how much I remembered from Mrs Oddly's 'This Is Our Country' project in Primary 5.

'A wall,' said Sputnik, 'eighty miles long.' He made the wall sound tastier than a cow full of ice cream.

Once the first fifteen cows were milked we let them out of the back door, which led straight to the pasture, then let the next fifteen through the big sliding door from the courtyard.

The moment we opened the door, Sputnik set off across the field towards the farmhouse.

'Sputnik! Come back!' yelled Jessie.

I went after him. Jessie tried to come too but the dad called her back to help him.

'That's so unfair,' she said. 'I milk cows and Prez goes off gallivanting with Sputnik.'

'The dog probably just wants to do his business somewhere,' said the dad.

'Exactly right,' said Sputnik. 'That man really understands me. I need a wee.'

– Go in the bushes.

'Oh no. No, no, no. I have big plans for this wee. Very big plans.'

9.
Chicken-and-Mushroom Pie

'An eighty-mile wall,' said Sputnik, as we walked into the farmyard. 'It makes you think.'

In Primary 5 Mrs Oddly had asked us to think about the wall. 'Consider,' she had said, 'how brilliant the Roman engineers must have been to build something so big and strong without machinery all those centuries ago.

'Think,' she said, 'about the moonlight flashing on the swords and spears of the Roman legion. Think of the blue paint on the bodies of the furious Picts.'

I knew Sputnik was not thinking about any of this. I knew exactly what Sputnik was thinking about.

'An eighty-mile wall!' he sighed. 'You could pee a good long message on a wall like that. You could pee a chuffing novel on a wall like that.'

– It's a long way off. Can you hold on till we get there?

'We've got transport – look.'

The little digger that the dad had been using to clear the farmyard was still out. The keys were even still in the ignition.

– No, no. We're not going joyriding. Besides, this thing only goes about two miles an hour.

'Have you read the instructions?'

– No. I haven't read the instructions.

'So how do you know how fast it can go? Let's take a look.' Sputnik walked once around the digger, then reached into his backpack and pulled out a massive hammer. *Clang!* He whacked the undercarriage of the digger.

– No. Sputnik. Please. They need this for the farm. You can't . . .

Clang! He whacked the other side. The digger rocked on its suspension.

'Get in!' said Sputnik.

– No.

'I'm not used to driving in this kind of gravity,' he said, ducking underneath the scoop. 'I think I should be under supervision. That means you.'

I jumped at the sound of a drill whistling somewhere under the scoop.

– Please stop messing about, Sputnik.

'Who's messing? I'm totally re-engineering this vehicle for the benefit of mankind.' He bounced into the cabin, pulled a few levers and brought the scoop down straight in front of us. It looked less like an elephant's trunk now and more like a rocket. From somewhere in his backpack he pulled out a circular saw and carved the front of the digger into a point.

'Nice job, Sputnik,' said Sputnik. 'OK. Let's start her up.' He turned the key in the ignition.

Sputnik has often tried to explain what happened next. It's all to do with physics. As you approach the speed of light, your body begins to lose mass. Or gain mass. Something like that. Anyway, you sort of stop being exactly solid, which means you can slice through traffic without bumping into it.

Whatever, just after he turned the ignition, the digger approached the speed of light. Less than a second later we were veering off a long straight road on to a car park fifty miles from Stramoddie Farm. My stomach, though, was still back in the farmyard.

A pair of buzzards circled overhead.

There was a smell of wet sheep, peat, coffee and cake.

See? I was even starting to notice the things that Sputnik noticed.

There was a sign pointing to a building with 'Visitor Information and Toilets' written on it. Behind the building a grassy bank ran across the top of the field. It had bits of wall sticking out of it. There were huge chunks of stone scattered all over the field. I'd never been here before, but I knew where we were. This grassy bank was Hadrian's earthwork. The chunks of stone were the remains of Hadrian's Wall.

A low, furious mutter came from Sputnik. 'That's the wall? That?! Is the famous wall?! Are you calling that a wall? That is not a wall. That is rubble. What's wrong with you people? You had a lovely long wall with nice big stones and you let it fall down?! Where's it all gone?'

I knew where it had all gone. We did Hadrian's Wall with Mrs Oddly in Primary 5.

– Over the centuries, farmers used stone from the wall to build barns and cottages and sheep pens.

'Oh, did they?' growled Sputnik, 'Oh, very did they? Well they can just chuffing well put them back.'

I should have worried when he said that.

I should have worried even more when he lowered the digger arm and drove over the car park, through the little wooden fence and up the hill towards the wall itself.

A lady in Roman clothes came out of the visitor centre, waving her hands in the air. At first I thought we'd time-travelled or that she was a ghost but she turned out to be just a guide in fancy dress. 'No, no, you can't bring that vehicle on to the site. The site is very fragile. This is an ancient monument. No diggers are . . . NO!'

The digger's spiky teeth and wide black mouth were bearing down on the lady, as though it was going to eat her. Sputnik was at the controls.

'NO!!' She jumped out of the way. Sputnik

scooped up a load of boulders from the field, then headed towards the ruins of the wall. 'What do you think you're playing at?!' screamed the Roman lady. She was looking at me. 'WHAT,' she yelled, 'is going on?'

That was a tough question for me. Because the truth is I had no idea what was going on. I had no idea how we'd even got there.

'Turn that engine off now! This wall is two thousand years old. It must be treated with respect.'

'We're going to treat it with respect all right,' said Sputnik. 'We're going to *mend* it.'

She was still looking at me. She couldn't hear Sputnik, though he kept on talking.

'I'm Sputnik Mellows. *The* Sputnik Mellows. This is a school project. My friend here was asked to imagine what Hadrian's Wall might look to Hadrian. I can tell you,' said Sputnik, 'he most certainly did not imagine it looking like this . . . mess. So we're fixing it.'

A man in a yellow hard hat and big boots and a high-vis jacket came striding out of the visitors' toilets.

'Excuse me!' the Roman lady shouted at him. 'Do

you know anything about this? Why is there a digger on the site?'

'No idea,' said the man in the hard hat. 'I'm Maintenance, so if anyone knew anything, it would be me. Responsibility for upkeep rests with the Department of Ancient Monuments. Not with a schoolboy in a digger.'

'Upkeep?!' howled Sputnik, 'Well, you haven't upkept it very well so far.'

'As far as we're concerned,' continued the man in the hard hat, 'you're a vandal. Get off the site right now, or legal proceedings will proceed.'

'Prez,' snarled Sputnik, 'is Hadrian's Wall important?'

– Of course it's important.

'Then why are these people leaving it lying around in bits on the ground? Either the wall is important, so they should fix it, or it's not important, so they should get rid of all these stones and have a nice field instead.'

The Roman lady screamed as the digger scooped up a load of stones, trundled up to the top of the bank and dumped them next to the wall. She screamed even more when it happened again. And again, until every stone in the field was piled up at the top of the earthwork.

He turned the engine off.

I could hear the Roman lady talking to the police on the phone. 'Not just any wall. *The* wall. Hadrian's Wall. The Roman wall. The Vallum Aelium. Our greatest national monument.'

Sputnik bounced out of the cabin, skimmed across the field and sat looking up at her. I assumed she was going to do some kind of citizen's arrest on him there and then. Instead she smiled and said, 'Now where did you come from? Aren't you lovely?' and ruffled his hair. She saw me walking towards her and snapped, 'Be warned, young man. The police have been informed. You are in deep, deep water.'

Sputnik handed her something that looked like a small pineapple. 'Ohhh!' she cooed. 'Is this for me?'

How could she be cooing at him – the actual culprit – while threatening me with arrest? There is no justice.

She felt the weight of the pineapple thing in her hand. Sputnik was still giving her that big-wet-eyes look. It looked weird on a wee alien with goggles but I suppose it looked cute if you thought he was a dog.

'I know,' she cooed, 'what you want.' She hurled

the pineapple high into the air. It arced towards the pile of stones.

'Good shot,' shouted Sputnik.

'Fetch! Go on, boy. Fetch!'

'FETCH?!' said Sputnik. 'Are you NUTS? That's a live hand grenade.'

– When you say live hand grenade . . .

'When I say live hand grenade . . .'

– What did you give her a hand grenade for?!

'We can discuss this later. For now, get your goggles on . . .'

– I haven't got any goggles. I'm going to be killed. We're all going to be killed! You said you were here to look after me! Now you're chucking live grenades around in my vicinity.

'Cover your ears. Get your head down. Five . . . four . . . three . . . DUCK!'

I threw myself on the ground and covered my ears. I did it so quickly that the Roman lady and yellow-hat man did the same.

Even with our ears covered, the noise was deafening. First came a thunderous sucking – as though a vast invisible cleaner was vacuuming the grass.

Then a terrible patter of pops like a massive

hedgehog rolling around on bubble wrap.

Then a whoosh as something flew past my shoulder. So close. So fast. I had to look up.

The grass was boiling like soup. Lumps and humps appeared in it. They sprang up and then they burst open. Rocks and stones erupted from under the soil as if pulled out by some giant hoover.

In computer games, when there's an explosion, all the pieces fly away from each other. This was an explosion, but a backwards explosion. Instead of flying away from each other, all the rocks were flying towards each other.

'Reverse dynamite,' said Sputnik. 'That stuff is literally the bomb. Just watch.'

With my hands over my face, peeping through the gaps in my fingers, I watched rocks, stones, bricks and lintels flock together, and swerve through the air. One by one they settled on the ruins of the Roman wall. They piled up on top of each other, shuffled along the wall, made space for one another, twisted into place. Dust billowed. The stones and rocks ground against each other. They clicked.

Then everything was still.

We could hear the buzzards calling again.

Sputnik shoved his goggles back on top of his

head and put his hands on his hips. 'Lady,' he said, 'Hadrian's Wall. As Hadrian meant it to be.'

A perfect, brand-new Roman wall stretched across the top of the field and away over the hill.

For a moment none of us said a word. Then the man in the high-vis jacket took his hard hat off and held it to his chest. 'That,' he said, 'is a fine piece of work.'

'Beautiful,' sighed the Roman lady. She sniffed and dabbed her nose with a bit of toga. 'The Vallum Hadriani.'

Then of course Sputnik went and peed on it. 'Got to sign my masterpiece,' he grinned. When he'd finished we all strolled along in the shadow of the ramparts for a while.

The man in the hard hat kept touching the stones, saying, 'Tidy bit of limestone. Looks good as new. Great piece of work. My name's Pavel, by the way.'

'Actually no,' said the Roman lady. 'When it was new, the milecastles at this end were originally made of turf and wood whereas that milecastle over there is . . . oh my!' She stopped. 'A milecastle! Come on! Let's go inside!' A little way ahead there was a stone tower sticking up out of the wall, with a pointy wooden roof and a kind of balcony. The Roman lady ran ahead and pulled at the door. 'It's open!' she whooped. 'Come on. I'm Emilia, by the way.'

We followed her up the wide, clean steps to the top of the tower and looked out.

That's when we saw it properly for the first time. The Wall. It snaked away from us, over the hilltops, in and out of valleys and into the blue distance. A tower rose up from the top of the next hill, as though the wall was sitting up and taking a look around.

'Oh. Now that's going to create a bit of awkwardness,' said Pavel, who was looking behind us to where the new wall went straight across the main road. The next milecastle stood just exactly where the central reservation had been. 'Looks is if you've closed the A7.'

'But it was worth it,' sighed Emilia.

A line of stopped cars stretched back along the road. Some of the drivers were turning around to go back the other way. Others were getting out of their cars to take a look at the wall. They patted the stones and walked up and down, as if they couldn't believe it was really there.

'Have to say,' said Pavel, 'in that toga, with the wall and the sunset and everything, you look every inch the Roman . . .'

'Roman what? Ruin?' she giggled.

'Goddess,' he muttered, then looked away, so they could each do their own private blush. He said, 'I suppose we'll be in endless trouble for disrupting the traffic?'

– Trouble? Of course we'll be in trouble.

'Trouble?!' Sputnik laughed. 'For fixing Hadrian's Wall? The nation will be insanely grateful. And anyway, if a huge fortification appeared out of nowhere, reaching from one side of the country to the other, who would think of blaming it on one boy and his dog?'

He was right. Ha!

People from the stuck cars strolled past us, gazing out over the fields and up at the battlements like dreamers. More of them came. They left their cars in the road and climbed up on the inexplicable wall. As the traffic jam got longer, people started to stroll across the fields towards the wall. Men from the roadworks in their yellow hard hats, families heading back from school with their kids in bright summer clothes, men and women on their way back from work, filming it all on their tablets and phones, the passengers from a big coach, a group of girls in tracksuits – looking down at them all, we felt like

Roman legionaries surveying the attacking hordes.

– Sputnik, you've caused a massive obstruction. You've built a wall across the main road.

'I didn't build it. It's been there for thousands of years.'

– But it's not been there for the last few hundred years.

'It was interrupted. Now it's gone back to normal, that's all.'

Pavel and Emilia were worried about the same thing as me. 'A lot of people,' said Pavel, 'are going to be very put out about this obstruction.'

'You're not suggesting that we knock it down?'

'Lovely bit of work like this? I couldn't bring myself to scratch it, never mind knock it down.'

'Sometimes an obstruction can be a nice thing,' said Emilia. 'You're going along in life, then something happens to make you stop and think and . . . everything looks lovely. Although it is getting chilly.' She was only wearing a toga. Pavel took his jacket off and draped it around her shoulders. Next thing I knew they were holding hands.

– We should be getting back to Stramoddie. The dad will be wondering where his digger is.

'If you like,' said Sputnik.

But somehow we couldn't leave. We carried on walking. Everyone carried on walking. The wall seemed to want us to walk on it, the way music wants you to listen to it.

We walked until the light began to fade and then a star appeared. Just one. Quite low in the sky, but very bright. If you looked closer, you could see that it was shimmering different colours. Everyone stopped to look at it, as though it was a light coming on in a window far away, calling them all home. I knew what it was. Sirius. The dog star. Sailors use it because it's nearly always the first star to come out.

'I'm not looking at Sirius,' said Sputnik. 'I'm looking at the tiny white star just next to it.'

I looked hard, but I couldn't see a tiny white star.

'One good thing about being a dog is their eyesight. It's a lot sharper than humans'. At night-time anyway. There's a little white star there. It's called the Pup. Look it up some time. It had a lovely little solar system.

All the time I kept looking where Sputnik was pointing. After a while I could just make out a tiny white star. After a while longer I think I could nearly see its planets swinging around it like sparks.

'My planet used to be third one along.'

– Used to be?

'Yeah. The Pup imploded. Became a white dwarf. All its planets were sucked into it. Now that whole solar system's not much bigger than a tennis ball.'

– But how come we can see it, if it's not there any more?

'You're seeing the light from that star. It's taken half a million years for that light to reach here, because it's half a million light years away. So when you look at that star, you're looking into the past. Half a million years into the past. A lot has happened since then. Now there's just an empty space where my home used to be. I've got nowhere to call my own in the whole of space. Imagine if every one of those stars was a party you're not invited to. Imagine every one was a door that won't let you in . . .'

I remembered the day they took Grandad away. The woman from the Temporary helped me pack my stuff and took me off in her car. In the rear-view mirror I saw the policewoman shut the door to Grandad's flat. I haven't been back there since.

– Don't you miss it? Home?

'Course I do. OK, maybe it wasn't the biggest planet in the universe, but it wasn't the smallest either. Had a lot of moons. It was nice to watch them following each other across the sky at night. It was, you know, home.'

– It was bad enough having to leave the flat in Traquair Gardens. I can't imagine what it would be like to have to leave your whole solar system.

'See? Even planets don't last forever.'

– You know, if we save the Earth, maybe you could stay here. Maybe you could live here. With me.

'I don't know.

– But we are going to save this one? I mean, Hadrian's Wall – that's got to be worth seeing. That is surely going in the *Companion*.

I finally felt we were beginning to save the planet.

'I don't think so.'

– But you loved it. You weed a message on it.

'But it also fell down. Imagine if someone came all the way across the universe to see the wall just because they'd read about it in the *Companion*, and when they got here there was nothing but a heap of rubble. What would people think? They'd think

Sputnik's Guide was an unreliable source and the Sputnik is not unreliable.'

We climbed back into the digger, turned the key in the ignition and one blink later we lurched to a halt in the farmyard.

The front door was open. We could smell the chicken-and-mushroom pie. And by the way, it tasted braw, even if it *was* the result of an armed robbery.

10.
Spanish Lessons

Normally during meals, everyone was talking at once. Like . . .

'No phones at the table.'

'I need to look up how to train a dog.'

'Magic wand!'

'Look it up after dinner.'

'No magic wands at the table.'

'Eat your peas.'

But that night Jessie didn't say a word. She stared sadly into her mashed potato as if it was a sleeping ghost. Without Jessie the conversation was more like:

'No phones at the table.'

'Eat your peas.'

Why wasn't she talking? Because she was too busy thinking about Sputnik and how he always ignored her and went off with me instead.

After tea Sputnik sidled in through the back door. Ray didn't notice because he was searching the kitchen for the TV remote control. The mum was busy checking her Facebook group for lost-dog notices.

Sputnik found the remote between the fridge and the sink and handed it to Ray.

'How did he even know I was looking for that?' said Ray. 'You know, I think Sputnik is unusually clever.' He flicked the television on. I was expecting the news to be all about the traffic congestion at Hadrian's Wall. I worried a bit that there might even be a film of us. But there was no mention of any of it.

'Looks like we got away with that,' said Sputnik.

The next few evenings Jessie got quieter and quieter. The gaps where she would normally talk got bigger and bigger. Then bigger. After a while you could hear people chewing. After a while more you could hear the cows chewing outside.

When people are talking I feel nicely invisible.

When it's quiet I feel everyone is looking at me. The silence was in my face like a spotlight.

There were a few days of school left before we broke up. I was thinking, If I don't say something, we are going to have a silent summer. I wanted to stand up and say, 'Please, please can you go back to yelling at each other?!'

Maybe I would have done that too, but one night while we were eating Ray looked over at me, winked and said, 'Did you all hear about Prez and the school alligator?'

Jessie looked up. 'There's an alligator in Prez's school?'

'Don't speak with your mouth full.'

'Aye. Would you credit it? Lives in the hot tub in the staff toilets. Anyway, apparently it got out, slithered into Learning Resources. School alligator opens its jaws and – *blurp!* – school alligator swallows the IT teacher while she's on the phone. And everyone is like, what are we going to do? Because no one knew what to do. But Prez jumps up on the table, prises its jaws open with the leg of a flip chart and helps her out. She was so pleased she gave him two merits.'

117

'Rayyy. Monnnd. Don't tease Prez.'

Jessie pointed out that me and Raymond didn't even go to the same school.

'It's all over Facebook. I swear he's practically a meme. Look! He's got the merits to prove it. Show her, Prez.'

The mum was looking at me. She was worried I was going to get upset. I rooted round in my backpack, got my homework diary and showed her two merits. As if that proved I'd wrestled an alligator.

Everyone laughed and I laughed too. And then they all went back to shouting just like before. I leaned back in my chair and just listened.

Amazing Stuff That Prez Did Today became a thing. Ray did a different story every night at dinner. Like the time he said I'd won half a million quid in the school casino.

'There's a school casino?'

'Yeah, don't you remember? Prez's school is the only one to have its own casino in the whole of southern Scotland. Anyway, the point is, Prez won half a million quid.'

'Prez's got half a million quid?! Really?'

'Not any more. He staked the lot on black

twenty-two. Lost the whole pile.'

I pulled out my pockets to show that they were empty, like they must have been full once.

All my days at school, other people had stuff I didn't have. They had nice phones. Proper sports kit. Brothers and sisters. Mums and dads. Now I had something no one else had. I had a friend who could float a shed on a gravity eddy. And light cigars with a lightsaber. Knowing I had Sputnik, I felt like the secret millionaire.

At school, other people had always had homework; I had work to do at home. I was learning things like how to cook, how to sort out Grandad's pension, how to answer all the letters he got from people he'd annoyed. The stuff you learned at school seemed far away and hard to do. But once you've learned to levitate a shed, lessons seem easy. It's like Sputnik said: just follow the instructions. I actually tried it in Spanish, which was the very last lesson before the holidays. Mr McAlister was handing out new textbooks for next year and doing his speech about how if any of us were going to Spain for a holiday we should take that opportunity to speak a bit of Spanish to a real Spanish person.

I went straight to the instructions – the bit at the

back with no pictures and rules about grammar and tables of verbs. Straight away the words there made me think of Grandad. He didn't speak Spanish to me at home, but loads of his favourite things had Spanish names: paella, tortilla, chorizo, *churros*, *cerveza*. The words and the rules just went straight into my head like a tune, then stayed there the way tunes do. When Mr McAlister asked a question – '*Como te llamas?*' – my hand went up.

'*Hola, me llamo Prez. Voy a pasar el invierno con la familia Blythe en una hacienda en Knockbrex, que se llama Stramoddie. Tengo un amigo nuevo. Se llama Sputnik; él también vive con la familia Blythe. Todo el mundo cree que él es un perro, pero no lo es.*' I was speaking Spanish, speaking it so quickly that even I couldn't understand what I was saying. Everyone was staring at me.

'*Hablas español con un acento excelente.*'

'*Gracias.*'

'How come he speaks Spanish really well but he never speaks English, sir? Is he actually Spanish?'

'*Prez, eres español?*'

'*¡Hombre! ¡Claro que no!*' I can't tell you what it's like to feel your mouth moving in the middle of your face, and to hear words jumping out of it and

120

Hola, me llamo Prez

bouncing around the room like foreign mice. '*Es que he leído las instruciones.*'

'No, he's not Spanish.'

'How come he talks Spanish so well?'

'He says it's because he's read the instructions. I guess he means the textbook. An example to you all.'

'Sir!' Murder Bell had his hand up. 'Sir, what's the Spanish for "Grandad", sir?'

'*Abuelo.* Can you say it?'

'*Abuelo*, sir. And what's the Spanish for "mad", sir?'

'*Tonto.* Why?'

'So "Mad Grandad" is *Abuelo tonto*. Is that right,

sir? What about "locked up", sir? How would you say, "Your mad grandad got locked up"?'

By now everyone in the class was giggling. They knew Murder was trying to wind me up.

The thing about Murder Bell is that he's in the Temporary with me. Only he doesn't want anyone to know. So he picks on me. How scared do you have to be to be scared that someone who never speaks is going to tell people that you're a Temporary Kid?

11.
Eggs

I did feel bad about Jessie. I really would have liked to tell her everything. But how could I? What could I say? 'Sputnik is not a dog. He's an alien. He can talk and he's good at fixing stuff. But he's fairly unpredictable and heavily armed. Plus maybe he'd like to play with you, but he really should be concentrating on saving the world.'

You'd think it would be easy enough to find ten things worth seeing or doing on Earth, but I couldn't guess what Sputnik would like. I really thought he'd love Hadrian's eighty-mile-long wall. But no. 'A wall's just a wall in the end. And walls fall down.'

– But you fixed it!

'I tell you what I liked. That yellow jacket that Pavel in the hard hat was wearing.'

– It was just a high-vis jacket like people wear

when they're doing roadworks or working on a ferry.

'Yeah. High-vis jackets. I've never seen them anywhere else in all the wide universe. I love the way it glowed in the twilight. That can go in the *Companion*. We can put it on the list.'

Last thing at night the dad would go round and make sure all the sheds and stables were locked up properly. I'd go with him and say goodnight to Sputnik. He'd always be lying in his hammock with his notebook, planning possible expeditions.

Sometimes Jessie would follow me over, with a plate of food for him. It seemed sad and wrong that I was talking to Sputnik about saving the entire world and she couldn't understand a word. After all, it was her world too. One night I thought, Whatever we do tomorrow, we should take her with us.

But Sputnik had other ideas.

1. Get up
2. Wash face with cold water (This stops you wanting to go back to bed)
3. Make bed (Then you can't go back to bed)
4. Brush teeth (Feels good)
5. Go (Breakfast can wait)

Sputnik had said we were going to make an early start. I was downstairs and ready to go by six o'clock. I'd forgotten that that's not that early on a dairy farm. I had my hand on the front-door knob when I heard the mum say, 'You're first out, Prez.'

She was looking at my backpack. I always keep it with me. But maybe she thought I was trying to run away. She said, 'A wee job for you. First out always brings in the eggs, OK? As many as you can get.'

When I lived with my grandad, he used to take me to school every morning and pick me up every afternoon, until the day when he didn't come. When I was at the Temporary, a minibus took us in the morning and brought us back after school. You couldn't get past the front door without a grown-up. So it felt amazing now to just open the door and be outside in the morning. The world looked different.

'The shadows are all pointing the other way,' said Sputnik. 'You normally don't see long shadows until the afternoon when they're going the other way because your sun is setting. In the morning, when it's rising, the shadows point east to west. Your brain noticed the difference but it didn't tell you. Let's go.'

– Can't we wait for Jessie?

'Time and tide wait for no man.' He waved a little book in my face.

– Where did you get that? That's my grandad's tide timetable.

'It tells you the times for high tide and low tide.'

– I know it does. That was in my bag. Look, it's got Grandad's name in the front. How did you get it?

'Stole it,' said Sputnik. 'Come on.'

We tramped across the pasture. Slowly this time, so the cows didn't get scared. When we got to the gate of the Coo Palace we stopped. There's a hedge there – a spiky one with little yellow flowers – and through a gap in the hedge something was shining. Bright blue.

'There it is,' said Sputnik. 'The sea.'

I knew it was the same place that we'd seen the other day – the Coo Palace was still there, and I could see the tops of the poles for the salmon nets – but it looked like a different country. The other day it had been flat mud with no sound except for some whistling birds. Today there was no mud – it was all waves crashing against rocks and seagulls screaming.

Sputnik licked his lips and rubbed his hands. For a minute I thought he was going to pick up the entire sea and swallow it like a pancake.

– I've never seen the sea before.

'What do you mean, you've never seen the sea? I thought you'd been all over the world with your grandad.'

– Yeah. Well, I mean, I haven't seen this bit of sea. Of course I've seen other seas. I've sailed all Seven Seas in fact. I just don't remember very well.

'What's this sea called?'

– I'm not sure. This is Rumblecairn Bay, so the sea must be . . .

'I'm going to call it the Punctual Sea, because it got here bang on time, according to your grandad's book.' He handed me back the tide timetable. 'How do they know what time it will come in?'

– It's all to do with the moon. The moon's gravity makes the water move around.

'That's something I love about this planet. Only one moon. No wonder you have the best gravity. We had a dozen moons where I used to live. Imagine that – a moon going past every half an hour. The tide was up and down like a frog on a frying pan.'

I'd never thought about that before.

'Definitely the tide is going on the list.'

We squeezed through the gap in the hedge and found a little sandy path that went along the shore – a sign said 'Rumblecairn Bay Caravan Site Only'. We strolled along it with the little waves swooshing next to us. It felt like we were taking the sea for a walk.

Sputnik made sure to stand between me and the water in case I got swept out to sea. 'It's my job to look after you, remember. You know,' he said, 'I'm really getting to like this planet. It'll be a real shame if we don't stop the destruction.'

Every time he talked like this, I looked up into the sky in case I could see the Destruction of Earth coming.

'Look at that! That is un-be-lievable!' Sputnik was standing very still, staring at a fat bloke with a walking stick who was leading a spaniel along the track towards the caravans. Every now and then he'd throw a rubber ball and tell the dog to fetch. I couldn't see much amazing about it.

'In all my travels,' he said, 'I've never seen anything like it. A dog that speaks English!'

– What makes you think it speaks English?

'He's talking to it and it's doing what he tells it to.'

– I don't know much about dogs, but I'm pretty sure they don't speak English. I think you can just train them.

'Train them to speak?'

– No, train them to, you know, fetch a ball.

Whenever the dog dropped the ball, the man picked it up and started going on about what a good dog it was and how it should keep away from the water and not touch the ducks. He even asked if it was starting to feel the cold and mentioned that it was colder today than yesterday.

'This doesn't look like fun for either of them,' said Sputnik. 'The big man doesn't want to throw the ball. The little dog doesn't want to fetch it. You're right. They're not communicating. They need help. They need *me*.'

He dashed off after them down the path. The man looked round when he heard us coming. He smiled at Sputnik, then looked at me and said, 'What's his name?'

'Sputnik,' said Sputnik.

'This is Figaro,' said the man.

'Sometimes you'd swear they could understand

every word you say,' said Sputnik.

'What breed is he?' asked the man.

'Tourist,' said Sputnik. 'Prez is my tour guide.'

'It's like he's really talking,' said the man.

Then he crouched down and he *barked – Woof woof woof* – right in Sputnik's face!!

'I'll tell you something for nothing,' said Sputnik. 'This joker is never going to learn to speak dog.' Then he strode off after the man's dog. 'If the man can't speak dog,' he said, 'then the dog'll just have to learn English for real. Hey, Figaro! Come to Sputnik!'

The spaniel scampered over and stuck his head up Sputnik's kilt.

'They're getting to know each other,' smiled the man.

I'm pretty sure sniffing someone's bottom is not good manners or the best way to get to know them. Sputnik didn't seem to mind though. They both ran off down the path towards the caravans. Then Sputnik rooted around in his backpack, pulled out a textbook and started showing the dog various pages from it.

'Here they come. Come on, Figaro. Come to Daddy!' called the man.

Figaro ran back to the fat bloke. Sputnik ran back to me, threw himself on the grass, pulled down his goggles and said, 'Sorted that out.'

Figaro was sitting in front of his owner with his head cocked on one side. 'Who's a lovely boy?' said the man.

'I am,' said Figaro. His voice was a bit like Grandad's – deep and rusty, like he'd had too many cigarettes – but he was definitely speaking.

The man looked sideways at me as though he was hoping we hadn't noticed. He said, 'Sorry about that. Just, errrm . . .' He picked up the ball and threw it, shouting, 'Fetch, Figaro! Go on, fetch!' as if nothing had happened.

'No,' said Figaro.

'Fetch,' said the man.

'No.'

'Go on, boy.'

'If you want it fetched,' said the dog, '*you* fetch it. I am done with fetching. If you want to keep the ball, put it somewhere safe. Stop throwing it away.'

The man was trying not to look at us. With his head turned to one side, he said it was nice meeting us and that he'd better be getting home now.

'That's right,' said Figaro. 'We're going back to

the caravan, to sit on the sofa bed and talk things over. If I'm going to carry on being your best friend, we need to get a few things straight.'

The man bent slowly down and tried to clip a leash on to Figaro's collar.

'Don't even think about it,' growled Figaro.

'How,' I said out loud, 'did you do that?'

'It's all in the instruction book.' Sputnik showed me the book he'd been reading to Figaro. *Dogs – A Companion* it was called. 'Why do people never read the instructions properly? You're never going to get the most out of things if you don't read the instructions.'

He swung the backpack off his shoulder, ready to put the book back inside, but then he said, 'Hard about! I almost forgot.'

'What?'

'This is no mere backpack for carrying luggage. This is my gravity ballast. The gravity's very different where I come from.'

I don't know much about gravity. For all I know they've got different gravity in France or China or wherever. But I do know that what he did next was unusual. 'Look . . .' I looked at his feet. They weren't quite touching the ground. 'Give me a shove.' I pushed his shoulder. He wobbled a bit, then drifted a few feet away, like a feather floating on a breeze.

'Gravity surf,' roared Sputnik, 'is up.'

Gravity surf?

'I told you. Gravity comes in waves. All you have to do is learn to ride the waves.'

He took the big pair of scissors from his belt and stabbed them into the mud. Then he lay down on the grass, with his hands holding the scissors, as if they were the steering wheel of a tiny car. He lifted one leg off the ground, then the other. Then he let go of the scissors with one hand and grabbed hold of his backpack strap. 'Now this –' he gasped – 'is the tricky bit. Can I do it? Yes, I can.' He pulled the scissors out of the mud with his other hand, grabbed the other strap of his backpack and now he was floating over the mud.

'Whooo, whoo. Come on, Prez!'

– I don't think my backpack works like yours. I just keep my stuff in mine.

'I keep my stuff in mine too. Have you read the instructions?'

– It's a backpack. It doesn't have instructions.

'So you haven't read the instructions?'

– No, but—

'Hit the deck.'

– Honestly I don't think it'll work. Plus shouldn't we be doing the list?

'You can use my scissors. It's all in the action of the scissors.'

I copied what he'd done. Got down on the ground, one hand on my bag strap, lifted one foot, then the other, then grabbed the other bag strap. And I was doing it. I was floating!

'Point your head where you want to go. And . . . kick like a frog!'

I'd had dreams about flying, but they were usually about soaring over rooftops and diving into clouds. I'd never even dreamed about what it would be like to skim over mud, slice through patches of dandelions at nettle height. Even though we were moving fast, I could see everything that was happening. Worms heaving themselves out of the mud. Centipedes and snails twisting between blades of grass, their backs gleaming. A spider stitching leaves together with its web. Drops of dew nestling in flower petals like light bulbs. Pollen swirling and glowing around my head. Bees bombing along next to me.

And then spray!

We were scudding over the water.

Oh. Over the water. What if we fell in?

'Just keep kicking your legs.'

A small wave smacked my face. Sometimes the sunlight sliced through the brown water so you could see fish flash, seaweed waving, ghostly jellyfish opening and closing. We swung around in a curve, speeding back towards the land. There was the red farmhouse in the crook of the green hill. And there

were the white caravans huddled like sheep. Cars stampeded by on the main road above.

I wanted to shout my name or just 'Yes!!!!' or 'Look at me!!!!' or something.

I looked across at Sputnik.

His head was up. His legs were kicking.

We were over the land now, skimming over the grass near the caravan toilet block.

'Tuck your knees in!'

I brought my knees up to my chest and straight away, tumbled over, landing flat on my back, looking up into the empty blue sky.

– Wow!

'Feeling hot?' asked Sputnik.

Now that he came to mention it, I did feel really hot.

'Stick your tongue out. Cool you down in no time.'

We lay with our tongues out, cooling down. It actually works.

'I did pick up one or two things from those dog conversations,' said Sputnik.

Puffs of white cloud were scattered around the blue like kites.

– That one looks like a giraffe. The four short bits are the legs. The long bit is the neck.

'Whoa! How did you do that? One minute it was just a clump of puffy steam. The next it's a sky-wide animal picture! That was genius.'

– I didn't *do* anything. I just *noticed* something. The cloud didn't change, just the way you looked at it. That one over there looks like a ship. See the sails? Or it could be a giant cigar.

'Whoa! Done it again. It looked nothing like a cigar, then you said it looked like a cigar and now it looks completely like a cigar just waiting for me to go up there and smoke it.'

– So . . . could this go on the list then?

'Yes!' He took out the red notebook and a pencil and wrote down 'Prez's Cloud Adjuster' – straight into the *Companion*.

– But I'm not adjusting the clouds, I'm just seeing them differently – the way I see you differently. Or the way Laika saw things differently. The things she said about Earth weren't wrong. They were just the way she saw them.

'You're right!' said Sputnik. 'Which means . . .'

He began rubbing out what he'd written.

– What are you doing?

'I can't put Cloud Adjuster on the list if there's no such thing as a Cloud Adjuster.'

It was horrible watching him make the list shorter when I'd only just made it longer.

– Couldn't you just put clouds on?

'Everywhere has clouds. Jupiter's got a red cloud the size of two Earths. It's not the cloud. It's the atmosphere. I don't know why more planets don't have an atmosphere. It makes such a difference when a planet has a duvet of breathable gases to snuggle down in. Think about it – lovely puffy clouds and mists and breezes and hurricanes – there's a whole circus of atmospheric fun whirling around your head every day.' He flipped his pencil again.

For once I felt like I was saving the world.

'Atmosphere. Third on the list. And now I need food.'

– Yes, let's go back to the house and get breakfast.

But breakfast in the kitchen turned out not to be what he meant by 'finding something to eat'. He dashed down to where the caravans were and . . . well, he bit a caravan.

He bit it on the front left-hand tyre.

Bit right through it. The tyre exploded. Scraps of rubber flew through the air like bewildered bats. Sputnik cannoned right into me. We went sprawling across the grass.

– What did you do that for? Why would you bite a caravan?!

'In the original *Companion*, it says everything on this planet is edible. Remember? You can eat anything on the planet.'

– What?! No no no. The only edible thing is food. And no one eats car tyres. Ever.

'I've eaten worse. Tangy. Want some?'

– No! I thought you were supposed to be looking after me. So far you've set off a hand grenade right in front of me, nearly blown me sky high with a tyre . . . let a little kid chop down a tree more or less on top of me and—

'Taken you gravity surfing. Come on. That was good.'

– . . . and put my entire planet down for shrinking. *Clang!*

I actually did think the world was ending there and then.

Without its front wheel to hold it up, the caravan slumped forward like an old grandad falling asleep in front of the telly. Its door fell open. A woman came out to see what was going on. A chair came tumbling out after her, nearly knocking her down the steps.

'Earthquake!' she shouted. 'Was that an earthquake?'

Even if I'd been really good at talking I could never have explained the link between the explosion, the flat tyre and the wee alien dog sitting in the road chewing a big chunk of rubber.

But I'm not good at talking. So we ran. All the way back to the farmhouse.

The mum was moving the cows out of the Coo Palace, back into the field. She stood on the drawbridge, waved at me and asked if I managed to get any.

– Any what?

'Eggs.'

I'd completely forgotten about the eggs. I looked at the floor and screwed up my eyes, ready to be screamed at.

'Look at you. Your feet are all muddy and your hair's all wet. Your T-shirt's torn. Where've you been? Were you looking for eggs in an eagle's nest?'

I wasn't sure that she'd understand if I said we'd been out surfing on gravity.

'Oh, Prez! You went to the shop, didn't you? You went down to the caravan site at Rumblecairn, to the little kiosk there. I didn't mean you to *buy* eggs.

We never *buy* eggs. I meant you to get eggs from the hens.'

Oh.

'Do you want to go and do it now? Ray will show you. Then it can be your job every day.'

That was the first time she'd given me a proper job. It felt good having something to remember to do. Like being back at Grandad's, where I had to remember to do everything.

To collect eggs straight from the hen, all you have to do is slip your hand under the hen and nudge her away. Really gently and smoothly so she doesn't notice it's happening. Ray showed me how to do it. I was slightly nervous.

'Don't be nervous. The hen can feel it if you're nervous and she thinks, I'm just a hen, so he must be nervous about something else like . . . FOXES!!! And she'll go off on a big chicken fear rampage. Feathers. Clucking. Fluttering. Hay everywhere. All the other hens catching the fear. You don't want to see that. So take a deep breath, think about something else and . . . good.'

I slid my hand under the hen. Felt the smooth shell of the egg. Still warm. When I opened my hand

and looked, the egg still had tiny feathers stuck to it.

'Yours was the best!' said Sputnik, when we carried the bowl of eggs back to the house. 'That chicken looked like it was going to explode! Loved it. Can you eat hens?'

'Yes, but not while they're alive, OK? And not while they belong to someone.'

'What do you do with the little round things you stole from them?'

– The eggs? We eat them.

'Go on then.'

– We eat them in the kitchen. You have to cook them first.

'Where do the eggs come from?'

– From inside the chicken. They've got baby hens inside them.

'The eggs come from inside the chicken?'

– Yes.

'But the chickens come from inside the egg?'

– Yes.

'So the chickens are in the eggs but the eggs are in the chickens? This is the most amazing thing ever.' He kept staring at the eggs. 'Eggs in chickens, chickens in eggs. The chicken is a magic bird. It's like the universe in feathers.'

– I think every bird does it, to be honest.

'What? No. That can't be right. Even ducks?'

– Even ducks.

In the kitchen, Ray cracked a couple of eggs on to the frying pan. Sputnik sneaked in to watch.

– You're not supposed to be in the kitchen.

'Come on! I have to see this. You might be looking at the fourth thing on the list.'

– So the Taj Mahal can't go on the list but eggs can?

'Let's see, shall we?'

I have to admit that when Ray cracked those eggs into the pan they did look good. Their yolks were bright yellow and round and, when they cooked, the whites were creamy white.

'Whoa!' said Sputnik. 'Are they going to turn into chickens now?'

– No. We're going to eat them on toast.

Ray put one on a plate in front of me. 'What d'you think?' he said.

They weren't just the best eggs I'd ever eaten, they were the best *thing* I'd ever eaten. Sputnik watched every forkful go into my mouth.

'Now the chicken is inside you?!' he gasped. 'This is just too much.'

'Look at this – Sputnik wants one!' Ray grinned. 'Here, Sputnik.'

Ray put a plate with one egg on it down in front of him.

'I couldn't eat that,' Sputnik said. 'That is a miracle of fluffy yellow engineering. I've got too much respect to put it in my mouth.' He pushed the plate away. Then he said, 'On the other hand, that does smell good.'

He wolfed three fried eggs.

That night I sat outside while Sputnik added eggs to the list and the ponies munched hay in their stables, as though they were thinking things over.

'I don't know what to put,' said Sputnik. 'Chickens or eggs?'

– Why not put both? The more we have the better.

It always felt special putting something on the list for the *Companion*.

'So far we have high-vis jackets, the tide, the atmosphere, chickens and eggs, your grandad's harmonica . . .'

– Really?!

'Don't you think the harmonica is amazing?'

– Not the way you play it. Wait till you hear Grandad on it. We'll have loads more ideas once I move back to his. That's where all the maps and stuff are.

'You're moving back to your grandad's?'

– Of course. As soon as he's sorted out.

Jessie was coming over with some leftovers for Sputnik.

– She saves half her dinner for you. It seems mean. Couldn't you say something to her, so that she knows you're not a dog?

But when she put the food down he rolled on to his back with his tongue hanging out and let her tickle his belly. She loved doing that. He pretended to love her doing it.

– You do realize that's just about the most doggy thing you could possibly do?

'She likes it.'

– But it's *doggy*. How am I ever going to tell her you're not a dog if you keep acting so doggy?

'I think in the days to come, when we're saving this planet, it might turn out to be really useful that some people think I'm just a dog.'

12.
Concealer

'Whose turn is it to
empty the dishwasher?'

'Where's Prez? He
can take Sputnik's
food out to him.'

'Shush, I'm trying to
listen to the weather.'

'Found my wand!'

'I'll take Sputnik's food.'

'Best if Prez does it.
He can get some eggs
while he's out there.'

'I want to do it.'

'But . . .'

'I'm doing it, OK?'

That was Jessie. She said, 'Sputnik let me tickle
his tummy last night. I'm finally getting somewhere with him so I should be feeding him from
now on.'

I was standing in the doorway. No one had noticed me yet.

'But Prez likes to do it,' said the mum, 'and it's good for him to have—'

'Prez is temporary,' said Jessie. 'He's going to leave soon. Sputnik is staying here for good. Sputnik's got to get used to me. Prez is just for summer. Sputnik is for life.'

I knew I was only staying for a while. I knew that. Probably not even the whole summer. Because if Grandad got himself sorted, I could go any minute. I just hadn't considered that it might mean leaving Sputnik behind, that's all.

The mum had seen me standing in the doorway. She knew I'd heard. She wished I hadn't. She acted like nothing had happened. She gave me a big smile and held Sputnik's bowl out to me. 'Morning, Prez, why don't you *and Jessie* take Sputnik his breakfast. Someone needs to turn out the ponies too. Oh. And eggs, please.'

I let Jessie carry the food.

She put it down in front of Sputnik. Sputnik was kind of horrified.

'What are you playing at? Bringing a woman in here when I haven't got my kilt on. And what's this?'

– Food.

He took one look at the gooey mess of dog food and said, 'I'd rather bite a caravan, thanks. I'll go in and fix myself some cheese on toast with Worcester sauce.'

– You're not allowed in the house.

'That's the legal position. But, you know, I have charm.' He put his head on one side and did that smile.

'He's not hungry yet,' said Jessie – something that was never, ever going to be true. 'Sputnik, want to come and help us with the ponies?'

'Are ponies edible?'

– No.

'You say that about everything. I'll come and see for myself.'

Jessie opened the stable doors, talking all the time. 'They love the sound of my voice. It keeps them nice and calm. They're not our ponies. We just look after them. The owners live in Kirkcudbright. They come here to ride them at the weekends and on Wednesday nights. They're called Mannie and Gallus – the ponies, I mean, not the people. Come in. It's a bit scary sometimes because the pony's so big and the stall's so little, but all we have to do is slip the bridle on, like that. Then clip the lead rein on, then we lead them out up the loaning and into the field.'

Sometimes a pony doesn't want a bridle on and jerks its head out of reach. Jessie showed me how to do this shuffle where you hold a carrot in one hand, and the bridle in the other. The pony goes for the carrot, and you swap hands at the last minute. You still give them the carrot. Quickly, before they get annoyed.

'They never mind really. I love it when you unclip the lead rein. They always go charging up the field as if they're late for something, like they've got to run to catch the pony bus. In the afternoon all you do is stand in the field with a carrot in your hand and they come trotting up. You clip a lead rein back on to the bridle and it just follows you back to the stall. I think maybe carrots have some kind of hypnotic ability when it comes to ponies.'

Sputnik followed us out of the yard and up the loaning. We were opening the gate to the field when Jessie noticed that he was missing. 'Oh no! Where is he? Please don't let him be up in the pasture scaring cows again.' We slipped the ponies' bridles and they cantered off up the field. 'You check the barns. I'll check the pasture.'

I ran off down the loaning. I knew he wasn't going to be in the barns or the pasture, or the shed or the stables. I knew exactly where Sputnik would be. The fridge.

Except he wasn't. The house seemed to be empty.

Where could he be?

'I'm upstairs.'

I was always surprised at how far away Sputnik could hear me thinking. If I'd shouted he probably wouldn't have heard me.

– You're not allowed upstairs. Come down.

'I'm hiding in the one place I know she won't look for me.'

– Where's that?

He was in Jessie's room.

– Come out. That's really bad. They'll all come back into the house when they've done their chores.

'I'm trying to save your planet. If she finds me, she'll put that thing around my neck and try and take me walkies. Every time I hear the word "walkies" I reach for my pistol.'

– But this is her room. It's private.

I didn't even want to look in. It felt wrong. But Sputnik wouldn't come out. He was lounging on

150

her bed, flicking through a book.

'Have you seen this?' He flipped it round so I could read the cover. It was a kind of scrapbook. It had 'Jessie and Ray' written on the front with a Sharpie, and the title . . . *Dogs of the Future*.

– That's really private. She didn't want me to know about that. Put it away.

But privacy is not one of the things that Sputnik cares about. He read the whole book out loud, holding up the pictures for me to see. I thought *Dogs of the Future* would be about robot dogs or dogs with superpowers. But it wasn't. The first page was a photo of a sheepdog. Underneath it said the dog was called Brach and it lived for eighty dog years at Stramoddie, then it died.

We asked Dad for a new dog. He said a new dog would just come into our lives one day. That's how it is with dogs. These are some of the dogs we hope will come into our lives in the future.

– Look! The dog in the picture is wearing the same collar that Jessie put on you.

'A second-hand collar! A collar from a dead dog! Unbelievable.'

– Maybe it means a lot to her.

The rest of the book was just pictures of dogs printed off the Internet. There were collies, Labradors, pointers, lurchers.

Then at the back there was a picture of a black-and-white dog wearing a little padded jacket and sitting in some kind of machine.

'That's her! That's Laika!' said Sputnik. 'What's she doing here?'

– Laika was a real dog?

'Of course she was real. I told you all about her. Look, that's her rocket. The Sputnik II.'

– I know. I just didn't expect her to be real like in a history book.

Underneath Jessie had written:

Laika
World's Most Famous Dog Ever
First Creature Ever to Orbit the Earth
First Earth Creature to Die in Space

'She did not die! That's a conspiracy theory. She was rescued by me and she had a grand old time, telling all kinds of lies about Earth.' He turned the page. Someone had drawn a square and written underneath in excitable marker pen 'Sputnik [awaiting photo] greatest dog ever'. The handwriting was the same but neater, more grown-up. Jessie must have written that bit recently and the rest years ago.

– She thinks you're the greatest.

'She's right about my greatness. Wrong about my species.'

– Shush.

Out in the pasture, the cows were mooing. The door from the farmyard opened. Water was being poured into a kettle. The noise of a car pulling up and chickens making a fuss. A visitor had arrived.

– Maybe it's Grandad? Maybe he's all sorted out and he's come to take me home in a taxi.

'I don't think so.' Sputnik was looking out of the window. 'It's a woman in a red VW.'

It had to be Mrs Rowland from the Temporary.

– Oh, well, that's just perfect. I'm supposed to be making myself useful. I'm supposed to be keeping you out of the house. And now she's here, you're not just in the house, you're in Jessie's bedroom poking around in her private things. This is so bad. We've got to get out of here . . .

'Fear not! The Sputnik has saved the day!' He had moved across to Jessie's dressing table and was holding up a tube of cream.

— What's that?

'Invisibilizer. According to the label it is scientifically proven to invisibilize for hours on end.'

— It's for covering up spots. It's skin cream. It hides your pimples. It doesn't make you invisible.

'Have you read the instructions?'

— It doesn't need instructions. It's cream. You rub it on. You wipe it off.

'You never read the instructions. "Total cover", it says on here. "One hundred per cent effective".' He was already rubbing it on my face.

— Stop it.

'Check out the mirror.'

— I looked in the mirror. I wasn't there. Even my backpack wasn't there!

'Now me,' said Sputnik.

I helped him rub it on and the two of us tiptoed downstairs. We could hear Jessie rabbiting on while the mum made Mrs Rowland a cup of tea.

'Dad has the radio on all the time for the news. He's scared of missing something. I don't know why. I don't know what he thinks he's going to DO about the war in the Middle East. Back in the day you never even knew there WAS a war until it was over and someone made a big tapestry about it. Instead of the radio blaring out, you'd just have the sound of some nice nuns doing needle-work . . .'

'I came to see how Prez was getting on.'

That was Mrs Rowland, shutting Jessie up. The

mum said she thought I was settling in nicely.

'Has he spoken yet?'

'Not really but then, as you can tell, we don't give visitors a lot of chance to talk.'

'Is he around now?'

'I think he's doing his chores,' said Ray. He was looking straight at me when he said that. I was standing right there in the doorway. 'Do you want me to go and look for him?'

He really couldn't see me. 'One hundred per cent effective,' said Invisible Sputnik.

– Could we put concealer . . . ?

'Right on the list.' I couldn't see his grin, but I could hear it.

I was so happy to get something else on the list that I didn't notice at first that they were talking about Sputnik.

'The thing is,' Mrs Rowland was saying, 'you never mentioned that you had a dog.'

Invisible Sputnik nudged me. 'Talking about me,' he whispered, 'the Greatest. I've probably won some sort of prize.'

'He's only recently arrived,' said the mum. 'He just turned up out of nowhere. We put a message on Facebook thinking someone would claim him. He must have a home somewhere. He's a very clever dog.'

'You call him Sputnik.'

'Yes we do. How did you know?'

'I friended you on Facebook, remember? Just seemed like a good way of keeping in touch. I don't know if you've seen any of the comments on your post.'

'No. No, I haven't checked.'

'There are quite a few. They're not about how clever he is so much as how dangerous . . .'

'Dangerous? Sputnik? Are you sure?'

'There's a man called Dmitri from Dmitri's shop . . .'

'The kiosk on the caravan site.'

'He says Sputnik came into his shop without supervision and acted in a violent manner.'

'Our Sputnik's soft as sponge cake,' said Jessie.

'I'm gentle as a cloud,' agreed Sputnik.

– Except you do carry a gun.

'Then there's the lady – also from the caravan site – who says he bit her caravan.'

'Bit?' said Ray. 'A caravan? Why would he bite a caravan?'

'Bit clean through the tyre apparently. She

thought it was an earthquake.'

'Why would he bite through a tyre?'

'I imagine it would be quite difficult to read the mind of any dog, let alone an unsupervised stray. What we *can* say is that he obviously has a very strong jaw . . . and is . . .'

'He's lovely. He lets me tickle his tummy and everything. He helped with the ponies this morning.'

'The hens aren't scared of him,' said the mum. 'That's usually a good sign of whether a dog has a nice calm nature or not. Hens always know.'

'Cows are scared of him though,' said the dad.

Everyone looked at him.

'It was all right in the end, but he did scare the cows.'

'Dad!'

'I'm just saying.'

'But *why* are you just saying? Sputnik is the greatest—'

'I took the trouble,' said Mrs Rowland, 'of ringing Dmitri in his shop, just to be sure. He did say the dog was very menacing indeed.'

'How was he menacing?'

'Dmitri wouldn't go into detail. But he was

obviously quite shaken. He said it was a terrifying encounter.'

– I told you not to rob shops at gunpoint.

'All this puts me in a difficult position. When we at the Temporary arranged for Prez to come and stay with you for a while, we had no idea that there was a dangerous dog on the premises . . .'

'But he's really, truly, not dangerous,' said Jessie. 'He's lovely.'

'. . . and if you'll just let me finish. If we *had* known there was a dangerous dog, we would never have agreed to let Prez come here.'

'But this is a farm,' said the mum. 'There are all kinds of beasts here. Always have been. We've had a temporary child every summer for years. We've got nearly fifty cows. There's a bull. He's dangerous if not handled right. And the hens could give you a nasty wee peck. You've got to expect animals on a farm. What difference does one dog make?'

'If it was your dog, it would be different. You could vouch for it. But this is a dog that turned up at your door just a few days ago. You don't really know anything about him. If the dog turned on Prez, then the Children's Temporary Accommodation would be held responsible.'

'But Sputnik *loves* Prez,' pleaded Jessie, 'and Prez loves Sputnik. He even slept outside with him a few nights back.'

The dad winced when she said that. 'We didn't make him sleep out. We didn't know he was sleeping out. He just did it.'

'They're best friends,' said Jessie. 'Sputnik likes Prez. He doesn't like the rest of us.' I could see that it really hurt her to say this. 'Please. Don't send Sputnik away.'

'I'm afraid it's either Sputnik or Prez,' said Mrs Rowland. 'They can't both stay here.'

So that was the choice. Me or Sputnik.

I was sure Jessie was going to choose Sputnik.

She wanted a dog.

They all thought he was a dog.

Like Jessie had said, I was going to leave soon anyway. They could have the dog forever.

'Are we going to vote on it?' said the dad.

'Of course we're not going to vote on it,' said Jessie. 'Can I just go and say goodbye to Sputnik?'

So they were going to let Sputnik go and keep me.

'That's surprising,' said Sputnik.

I was surprised too. If things had been different it would have made me happy, I think.

The dad rubbed Jessie's hair as she went by. She was crying. He pulled her in for a big hug.

She wasn't going to find Sputnik outside though. We were already running away.

13

Post-It Notes

All the time I was at Stramoddie I never unpacked my backpack, just in case. Now this had happened, I didn't have to pack. We just went.

Across the road from the top of the loaning there's a bus stop. It's just a wooden hut painted blue with pictures of gannets and seals, but it has a seat inside. We hid in there. It was cosy and dry. I thought about living there until Grandad came to find me. But Sputnik reminded me we still had a planet to save.

I had the key to the flat in Traquair Gardens.

– We could go back there and hide.

'It can be our secret HQ for saving the planet,' said Sputnik. 'Have you got money for the bus?'

– I totally forgot about the bus fare.

'Don't worry, I'm going to show you how to stage

a simple ambush. We'll hijack the bus and then we can go wherever we like for free.'

It was only when I turned round to answer him that I saw we weren't alone at the bus stop.

Jessie was sitting on the bench. I knew from the way she looked straight at me that the concealer had worn off. 'I knew you'd be here,' she said.

How did she know we'd be here?

'Where else would you be? If Sputnik can't stay, I don't want to stay. I knew that you'd feel the same. But you can't just run away from Stramoddie. It's too far from anywhere. If you're going to get away you need to take the bus. Where are we going?'

WE?!

'Let me guess. Your old flat in Dumfries. Where else could you go? Great. We'll hide there until your grandad's sorted out. I bet *he'll* let us keep Sputnik.'

– What!? Why do I always end up looking after people? First it was my grandad, then it was you and now it's Jessie.

'You've got a kind face,' said Sputnik.

She must have seen me looking annoyed. She said, 'Have you got the bus fare?'

I shrugged a no.

She put her hand in her pocket and pulled out a clump of five-pound notes. 'Bought three calves on Fair Day. Birthday money. Raised them myself. Sold them last week. This money is all mine. You need me. I am the money.'

She was right that we couldn't have run away on foot. The bus took forever. It snakes through the lanes and across the bridge into Kirkcudbright. It sat in the car park by the quay for a while. Jessie's phone rang.

'My mum,' she said, and turned it off.

Then we went through woods, across the big road, into more woods, down more lanes for hours. The first thing I recognized was the giant Tesco on the bypass as you come into Dumfries.

From there we headed into town.

Jessie put her face against the window. 'So many streets,' she said. 'How are you going to know which one is yours?'

– As if I'd forget my own street.

The thing is, though, Dumfries did seem loads busier and sound loads noisier than I remembered. Down at Stramoddie, there's a lot going on but it's all about one thing – cows. Cows being milked, cows being born, cows being taken in, taken out, bought and sold. Here there were all kinds of different things happening – all at the same time. Kids playing. People shopping. People cleaning the streets. Someone repairing the bridge. When we got off the bus, I grabbed hold of Jessie's hand to make sure she was all right.

'Get off,' she snapped. 'I have been to town before you know.'

– Oh.

'I came for the Agricultural Show and it was way more busy than this. There were cars everywhere. And tractors. And a bloke with a camel. This is quiet compared to then.'

We walked over the footbridge and along by the Robbie Burns Centre. We got to the flats. Ours is number 4.

It was only when we arrived that I realized how long it had been since I was there. I'd always thought of 4 Traquair Gardens as home. But can a place still be home if you haven't seen it for ages?

Mrs Mackie was smoking a cigarette out of the window of her flat when I walked up. She waved at me and asked how Grandad was. She seemed pleased to see me. Somehow it made me feel better, like I really was coming home. I put the key in the lock. It went in but it didn't turn. I jiggled it. It still didn't turn.

'I can sort that out,' said Sputnik, fastening the chinstrap of his flying helmet.

– No explosives, please. No guns and no . . .

He was gone.

The bathroom window was slightly open. He'd leaped up and squiggled through it. A few moments later we heard him strolling down the hallway. He opened the door from the inside.

'See? He's a clever, clever dog,' said Jessie. 'How could they say he was violent?'

– If only you knew.

'Is this where you used to live?' she asked as we went inside.

– No. This is where I *do* live. Where I'm going to live. With Sputnik.

'I don't think so,' said Sputnik.

But obviously she couldn't hear my thoughts and she couldn't understand Sputnik. So she just went inside.

Everything was different. The hallway used to be decorated with blue wallpaper. Now the walls were bare and the old wallpaper lay in big curls along the carpet. Someone had scraped it off.

In the living room there was no furniture. Just a pile of boxes shoved into one corner.

In my bedroom – no bed. No carpet. No bookshelves. No wardrobe.

'It's a bit . . .' said Jessie, trying to think of the right word, 'bare. Where did you sleep?'

There was a brand-new mattress propped up in the corner, still in its plastic, and the pieces of a new bed still in its box.

Grandad's bedroom used to be so full of stuff you could hardly get in. Now there was a pile of wood under the window, which I recognized as his old wardrobe and desk, but taken apart. All his clutter was piled up in a corner, stuffed in bin bags. Under the bin bags I could see a wooden box with metal corners. Grandad's sea chest! I'd found his sea chest. Piled up with rubbish. That was just wrong. I tried dragging it out. Jessie came to help me.

'Prez,' she said, in a low, quiet voice as if she was worried that there might be someone in the next room, 'you know what's going on here? Someone else is moving in. New people. They're throwing all your stuff out. That's not nice.'

– No. It's not nice.

'Prez, you don't live here any more.'

I tried opening the chest, but it was locked. I suppose Grandad had the key. I took some Post-it notes and a Sharpie out of my bag, wrote a note and stuck it on the sea chest:

IMPORTANT STUFF.
NOT YOURS.
THIS IS OURS.
LEAVE ALONE.

'Post-it notes?' said Jessie. 'In your bag? Oh. Does that mean . . . the ones in the bathroom – are they yours? Did you stick those up?'

I used to stick Post-it notes on things to help Grandad remember stuff. There were still some on the mirror and the cistern in the toilet. Some on the backs of doors and a lot still in the kitchen.

Eat breakfast
Brush your teeth
Do not go out
without trousers
Check your trousers
are fastened

'I've never met anyone who needed to be reminded to wear trousers.'

Leave the galley
shipshape
Don't abandon ship
without your keys
Sleep in your
cabin – not in
the toilet

Don't capsize
the bins
You are not in a
ship (you are in a
house in Dumfries)

'I never met anyone who needed to be told a house is not a ship before. Were you really confused when you lived here, or what?'

Then she found one stuck to the bedroom door. It was a school photograph of me, with a note stuck to it that said:

This is Prez. He is your grandson. He is not your brother or your mate Sergei from the engine room.

'Oh, I get it now,' said Jessie. 'You didn't write these for *you*, did you? You wrote them for your grandad. To help him remember stuff. Jeez, he must have been really forgetful. You don't think . . . maybe he just moved house and forgot to tell you?'

She was so wrong I actually laughed. She laughed too.

Then she went to the front door and shouted up at Mrs Mackie, who was still smoking out of her window, 'Excuse me, do you know what happened to old Mr Mellows? Is he no coming back?'

'Sandy? No, Sandy won't be coming back, hen. Prez will tell you. The police came and took him away.'

'The police?'

'Aye. In a police car. They put him away, and not before time.'

It's a funny thing, but I'd forgotten everything about that day. Now that she said it, it all came back to me. The sirens. The woman police officer. Me wondering whether I should run away or maybe hide. Of course they put him in prison! It was during his shouting-at-the-telly phase. He'd somehow got into Mrs Mackie's flat and started shouting at her telly. When she asked him to stop he said, 'Sorry, I got confused. Shall I show you how to chop carrots really fast? Pay particular careful attention.'

He'd barely got his wee chopping knife out of his top pocket, where he always kept it, when Mrs Mackie shouted, 'Oh my God, he's got a knife!' and Mr Mackie called the police.

They locked Grandad up. Of course they did. How had I forgotten that?

He was never coming back.

Look at the flat.

There was nowhere to come back *to*.

'So your grandad's in prison? Did you not know?'

'Aye,' I said, 'I ken that. I just forgot about it.'
And suddenly there I was, talking.

I started to tell Jessie everything about him. How at first it was just little things, like he would make a pot of tea but forget to put the tea bags in. Or he would forget which day it was. Or whether it was morning or night-time.

'Then he took to going off on big walks. At different times. I thought he was just wandering, you know, not knowing what he was doing. But then I found a tide timetable he'd left in the toilet, with the times of high tide underlined. And I figured out what he was doing. He was going out every day at high tide. So I stuck the tide timetable up on the kitchen wall, and a few minutes before high tide every day I would say, "OK, Grandad, time to go and see if there's any ships in." But there were never any ships in because there are no ships on the River Nith. But still he liked the walk. We'd get down to the footbridge and I'd say, "Och, Grandad, we just missed the boat!" And he'd say, "Never mind," and tell me about one of his voyages.'

'What if you were at school?'

'Oh, that was the worst. First time he rang me in school I wasn't that bothered. He said the electricity had gone and he needed me to come back urgently, it might be engine trouble. I sneaked out

172

just after registration. When I got home he said, "Come in, come in. It's really dark."

'"That's because the curtains are closed," I said. I ran my hand along the wall. I found the light switch. I flicked it. All the lights came on.

'"Smooth work, sailor," he said. "You're the best electrician in port. Have you got a business card?"

'"Grandad it's me, Prez." He'd completely forgotten who I was.'

'That must have been hard,' said Jessie.

'It didn't stop him ringing me up all the time,' I said. 'One time he called me during break and said, "Is that the electrician?" And I was like, "No, it's your grandson." He said, "They're trying to kill me."

'"Who's trying to kill you? Where are you?"

'"I'm not sure. I've lost my bearings."

'"How can I come and get you if I don't know where you are?"

'Then he said, "This is a distress call. Mayday, Mayday." The phone started to bleep. I think he was tapping out Morse code on the buttons.

'I had to shout, "If you're in danger, you need the police. Not an electrician."

'"They're trying to kill me. Using electricity."

'I had to get him to describe where he was. He was stuck on the central reservation on the bypass just past Homebase.

'I said, "They're not trying to kill you, Grandad, they're just driving past. They don't expect to find an old sailor wandering around." So I went and got him.

'He never threw anything out. You could hardly see the bed. The room was rammed with stuff. Piles of magazines were sliding into each other. There were stacks of boxes with words Sharpied on the sides, like "shoes", "maps", "memories" and – this was a bit strange – "teeth".

'"I get confused," Grandad said, "about what's important and what's not. So I keep it all." He looked around the room. "The really important things I keep in my sea chest, but –" he carried on looking around the room – "I don't know where the sea chest is." He looked at me. "Prez," he said, "I fear I am adrift."

'I'd say, "Don't worry, Grandad. I've got the helm. Just like you had on the night the iceberg came."

'He'd say, "Just don't let them set me down at Shangri-La, eh?"

174

'I didn't know what he was talking about. Maybe I should have called for help then. But I was worried they'd take him away. So I kept on covering for him. And then they took him away anyway.'

That was the most I'd spoken in ages. It might be the most I'd ever spoken. It was definitely the saddest thing I'd ever said. So you can see why I was a bit surprised to look up and see Jessie laughing at me.

'Why are you laughing?'

'Your accent.'

'What about my accent?'

'You sound just like an ordinary person. Like someone from round here.'

'I am an ordinary person from round here.'

'Aye, but . . . we didn't think you were. You never spoke so, you know, that was mysterious. Except that time in Spanish. So we thought maybe you were Spanish. Or Mexican. And you're good with animals.'

'I'm good with animals? Really?'

'Aye! Most of the Temporary Kids, they run a mile when they see a cow. You were there washing udders and collecting hens' eggs. You've got a gift. You even calmed the cows down when they were all stampeding.'

'That was actually me,' said Sputnik, swanning into the room half covered in curls of old wallpaper.

'And the dog, of course,' said Jessie. 'The dog seems to understand every word you say . . .'

'He doesn't say any words,' said Sputnik.

'. . . or at least every word you *don't* say,' said Jessie.

We were in my bedroom then. Or what used to be my bedroom. I tried to put everything back the way it was in my head. The wardrobe. I had a lampshade that looked like the moon. Where was that? I had photographs. How could anyone just take your photographs? It was like a bomb had gone off in there. Like a bomb had blown up everything I had.

'Prez,' said Jessie, 'this is not your house any more. We probably shouldn't even be here. We've got to go.'

She had thirteen missed calls from her mum.

So we went back to the farm. It wasn't like there was anywhere else to go.

14.
31 July – St Peter's Summer Treat

It was late when we got back. Almost dark as we walked down the loaning. They obviously knew that we'd tried to make a run for it. But they didn't say anything, just served the tea.

'We've been thinking about the best thing for Sputnik,' said the mum, 'and for all of us. And we've decided it's just not right to send Sputnik to the animal rescue.'

'Yay!' whooped Jessie. 'So Sputnik is staying here?'

'Well, not quite. We're going to have to send him away, but not very far. The McCrimmins are going to take him.'

The McCrimmins were the people who owned the ponies.

'The McCrimmins?! They've got everything already. They've got a trampoline! And they've already got dogs. They've got *packs* of dogs.'

'So Sputnik will have lots of company. It'll be nice for him.'

'They live in town. How can it be nice for a dog to live in a town?'

'They live in Kirkcudbright,' said the mum. 'It's only just up the road. You'll be able to see Sputnik whenever you like.'

'They're coming over to the Hayfield on Sunday. We'll hand him over then.'

The Hayfield wasn't just a field with hay in it. It was a thing. 'Back in the day,' the dad said, 'when they brought in the hay the fields would be full of folk. Singing and laughing. And when the work was done, the farmer's wife would lay out a big tea in the field. Now you never see a soul in the fields. It's all machinery. And no one does the hay, only the silage in the big black bin bags.'

'But we still do a Hayfield treat. Our church is over in Kirkcudbright. Once a year I mow the bottom field and everyone from the parish comes down. And the people from the caravan site come up. We make a hay castle out of hay bales. There's races and flags and stalls. It's all in a good cause. We call it the St Peter's Treat. You'll love it, won't he, Jess?'

'You are sending Sputnik away,' said Jessie.

'Yes, but not to—'

'You're sending him away.'

'Not *away* away. Not like—'

'You're sending him away. Say it.'

'I'm sending him away.'

On the morning of the Treat I collected the eggs and went down to the stables to see Sputnik. He wasn't there. He wasn't in the kitchen or the hallway. In the house there was nothing but Blythes shouting:

'Hurry up!'

'We've got to get the place ready before the people come.'

'Don't wait for me. Just go.'

'No. Come now. You've got jobs to do.'

'I'm not ready.'

'You don't need to be ready. The field needs to be ready.'

'Where's Annabel?'

'Here we are!'

Annabel appeared at the top of the stairs.

Jessie was standing next to her.

Sputnik was behind them.

'What. On. Earth – have you done to that poor dog?'

'Dressed him up!' whooped Annabel.

'If he's going away,' said Jessie, 'he's going away in style.'

Sputnik wasn't wearing his usual flying helmet. His hair was curled up on top of his head in thick ringlets. More ringlets were piled up like a big hairy crown, all tied together with ribbons. Three ribbons. Sparkly ones.

'You used curling tongs on the dog?'

'Curls!' trilled Annabel.

'Oh, please tell me . . . no . . . really . . . you haven't . . .' The ribbon was not the only sparkly thing about him. 'You've painted his toenails?'

'Shiny!' explained Annabel.

'Attractive,' said Ray, 'but inappropriate.'

'Cruelty. Pure and simple. Poor thing.'

'Let's get those ribbons off for a start.'

The dad reached up to undo the ribbons. Sputnik threw his hands up to stop him.

'He likes it!' whooped Annabel.

'No one,' snarled Sputnik, 'touches my ribbons.'

'He likes it all!'

'I,' said Sputnik, 'look amazing.'

The dad hitched a wooden trailer piled with hay bales on to the back of the tractor. We all climbed up and sat in among the bales while the tractor trundled down to the bottom field. There were some flags and a tent, a long wooden table and a pile of chairs.

'Now we've got to make the table look nice.'

'Everyone is staring at the dog.'

'We need a finishing line for the races.'

'Where's the guy with
the loudspeaker?'

'Couldn't you at least take
the nail varnish off?'

'The McCrimmins are doing the pony rides at the
bottom end. So the hay castle goes up here.'

They all seemed to know what they were doing.
They did it every year. They were a team. I got left
behind with Annabel, Sputnik and a cartload of hay.

– We have to stop them sending you away.

'Dead right we do,' said Sputnik. 'Otherwise
your wee planet will soon be even more wee.'

– Couldn't you just show them that you're not a
dog?

'That's not up to me. That's up to them. All I
can do is keep being amazing and hope that someone
figures it out. Come on.' He leaped up on the trailer
and put his back to one of the bales.

'Come on! Keepy up! Don't let it hit the ground.
Find the gravity stream and let it float.' The bale
didn't fall off the trailer. It drifted gently towards
the ground like a deflating party balloon. You could
pat it through the air, send it whichever way you
liked with a touch of your hand, make it rise a bit

further into the air with a poke of your knee.

'Magic Sputnik!' yelled Annabel.

Soon we had a system going. Sputnik floated bale after bale off the side of the trailer and I poked and patted and guided them through the air until they landed in the right place. I soon figured out how to land one on top of the other and another on top of that, so we could build really high walls. It was like herding helium-filled sheep. We stacked them higher and higher.

'Nearly done!' shouted Sputnik as one more bale drifted by. I picked Annabel up and popped her on top of it. She giggled and squealed as I shepherded it up towards the top of the castle.

'Last one!' called Sputnik. I jumped on that one myself and steered it with my feet, like a skateboard. On floating bales we chased each other round the battlements of the hay castle, then down to the ground past the sweet-smelling walls. It was only when we landed and looked up that I realized what we'd done.

– Sputnik! It's leaning!

'It's supposed to be. Look! You've built the Leaning Tower of Hay.'

– How will it stay up?

'Same as the Leaning Tower of Pisa.'

'How . . . what . . . how did that happen?' Ray had come back. He stared up at the castle. 'You didn't do that, did you? Not on your own. Who helped you?'

'Magic Sputnik,' said Annabel truthfully.

'Mum! Dad! Come and see what Prez did!'

'Best we've ever had.'

'But how on earth . . . ?'

'Magic Sputnik.'

'Wow!'

There was tug-of-war for tractors. A hook-a-duck stall and a coconut shy. Someone with two pet owls. Donkey rides. A burger van.

And there was a dog show.

Jessie had wanted to enter Sputnik, but Sputnik entered himself. He walked up to the judges and looked at them with his head on one side.

'Oh, aren't you lovely?' said the judge whose jumper was decorated with hundreds of little begging dogs.

'What breed?' asked the judge in the tweed jacket.

'Explorer,' said Sputnik.

'Mostly lurcher, we think,' said Jessie.

'And genius,' said Sputnik.

'But sort of collie-ish too,' said Jessie.

'And aviator,' said Sputnik. 'Probably the greatest aviator.'

'I'll put him down as indeterminate,' said the first judge, licking the end of his pencil. 'Age?'

'About a billion years old,' said Sputnik. 'Give or take a millennium or two.'

'Eight,' said Jessie.

'I was talking in dog years,' said Sputnik. 'I'm not a dog.'

'Does he have any special abilities?'

Sputnik's special abilities scrolled through my brain – gravity surfing, the shop-robbing, his amazing ability to get the most out of an instruction manual.

'Very good at finding the TV remote control,' said Jessie.

'Any special notes?' said the judge.

If he'd asked me I would have had to say, 'Not actually a dog.'

– Entering a dog show when you're not actually a dog is surely cheating.

'You're like a dreich day in Dunoon,' laughed

Sputnik. 'If folk insist on thinking I'm a dog, the least they can do is give me a prize for it.'

Everyone was clapping as Sputnik and the dogs took up their places. One of the other dogs was Figaro. Sputnik said hello to him, but he never replied. The judge with the doggy jumper said, 'First test will be to see how many times you can make your dog fetch in a minute. Owners, please take a stick . . .' He handed out some sticks. Jessie waggled her stick in Sputnik's face.

Sputnik looked at me and said, 'I'll sit this one out.'

– Jessie will be really sad. Go on, just for her.

'And . . . go!'

Owners threw sticks. Dogs flew after them. Owners threw sticks again.

'Go on, Sputnik, go on! Fetch!' yelled Jessie increasingly desperate.

'I've said it before and I'll say it again,' said Sputnik. 'Sputnik does not fetch.'

'*Sput-nik!*' howled Jessie. People were laughing now. She was going red. Tears sparked in her eyes.

One other dog wasn't fetching properly, some kind of mini sausage dog. Is there such a thing as a cocktail-sausage dog? Basically it was too little to carry its stick, but its owners weren't having that. They were two massive stubble-headed lads in Queen of the South tops. One of them put his fingers in his mouth and whistled so loudly that it drilled my eardrums. It impressed everyone except the cocktail-sausage dog, which just lay down and rolled over.

'How is he doing that noise?' asked Sputnik, looking up at Jessie.

'Come. On. Sputnik. PLEASE,' pleaded Jessie.

I suppose when the people looked at Sputnik all they saw was a very disobedient dog, but I don't know what they saw when he did what he did next. They were definitely impressed though.

Sputnik put his fingers in his mouth, stretched his lips and whistled loud and long. I don't know what anyone else saw, but I know what they heard. They heard a dog whistle.

The other dogs stopped fetching.

The owners stopped throwing.

Everyone just stared at Sputnik.

He whistled again.

'Love it,' he said.

'Amazing,' said the judge. Then he asked Jessie how she had taught him to do that.

Jessie shrugged. 'He's a clever dog.'

'I just love to learn new skills,' said Sputnik.

'Extremely impressive,' said the judge. 'But he failed to fetch any sticks, so he has lost this round.'

Figaro won the stick fetching. He had fetched ten times in one minute.

'You disappoint me greatly, Figaro,' said Sputnik. 'You have a servile attitude.'

Figaro whimpered.

'Don't whimper. I know you know what I'm saying.'

After that it was the obstacle race. The dogs were supposed to run up a short ramp, jump through a hoop and then through a little tunnel, pick up a beanbag and run back to their owners.

They used a starting pistol for this one. Sputnik was interested in the pistol but not in starting. He had got a taste for applause though, and when he saw the hoop on the obstacle course . . . well, I'll just say . . .

Hula-hooping.

Everyone went crazy. Even the competing dogs seemed impressed.

'That is no way a dog,' said the Really Big Lad.

'How can that be a dog?'

It was the first time I'd ever heard anyone else guess that Sputnik wasn't a dog. So I was interested.

'Of course he's a dog,' said his mate.

'Dogs can't hula, so he can't be a dog.'

'What else could he be?'

'A robot?'

'Of course he's not a robot. Look, he's wearing nail varnish.'

'I don't know what he is, but I do know the owner's a cheat.'

'Sputnik here is very talented,' said the judge in the jumper, 'but sadly we must disqualify him, as he did not complete the course. Also, he's distracted the other dogs. Which was not very sportsdog-like.'

'Because it's an evil robot,' agreed the Really Big Lad.

So Sputnik didn't win.

'The winner is the delightful little sausage dog of Mr Jez and Mr Ed Armstrong.'

'YEEESSSSSS!' screamed the Really Big Lad (who turned out to be Jez) as the judge handed them their prize – a tiny silver egg cup and a massive haggis.

'YESSSS!' screamed the other one, holding the

haggis in the air like it was the World Cup. Then they both started chanting, 'Champions!' and running round, each of them holding one handle of the tiny cup.

I looked over at the dad. He was talking to Mr McCrimmin. I knew in my heart that whistling and hula-hooping were not going to keep Sputnik at Stramoddie. I went back to the Leaning Castle of Hay.

I drifted round the top of the tower on the floating bale, watching all the fun. I could see a lot of people fussing around Sputnik and Jessie. But really I was watching the dad talking to Mr McCrimmin. Mr McCrimmin kept nodding his head. He shook hands with the dad. Then he did this terrible thing. He bent down and he scooped up Sputnik, stuffed him under his arm and walked off with him.

I could see Sputnik's feet kicking as though he was trying to swim out of it. I could hear him shouting, but I couldn't hear all the words. But I could clearly make out one: 'PREZ!!!'

The moment he shouted, my floating bale stopped floating. I hit the floor in a shower of straw. When I looked up, Annabel was looking down at me, pulling my shirt and shouting, 'Sputnik gone!

Sputnik gone!' Ray came running over. He picked her up, but she just yelled, 'Want Sputnik! Want Sputnik back *now*!'

'You're all right. All right. You're not cut. Just a fall. Are you all right, Prez?'

I didn't move.

'Want SPUTNIK!'

'Shush, Annabel. Prez, are you all right?'

I lay among the ruins of the bale, like a shattered bird's nest. All I could picture was Sputnik's legs frantically kicking the air as the man carried him away. I'd never fly on a bale of straw or use my backpack to skim across the sea, ever again.

When everything was tidied away, the mum and the dad counted all the money into a shortbread tin. The dad said, 'Give yourselves a big pat on the back. You've helped raise more than two thousand pounds for SCIAF.'

No one patted themselves on the back.

'You're helping to make a better world. Leftover pies and sausages from the sausage-and-pie stall for tea.'

The world! I was so sad about Sputnik I'd forgotten to be worried about the world. How was I going to help him save it now?

I tried to make my thoughts go loud inside my head, hoping that he could hear them even though he was on the far side of two big hills and a river. I listened out for some sign from him.

There was nothing but the chink of knives and forks on the plates. Nobody spoke. It was like a whole family of Prezes was sitting round the table.

Suddenly Jessie slammed her fork down and said, 'I don't think Prez should go away.'

Everyone stared at her but I stared the most. I'd thought she was upset about Sputnik, not about me.

'Jessie . . .' said the mum.

'It's not fair! Prez has got nowhere to go away *to*. Just the Temporary. He can't be temporary forever. He has to be permanent somewhere. Can't he be permanent here?'

'Now, Jess, you know that's not what we do. People come for the summer. They have a good time. Then hopefully they find somewhere. You know that.'

I smiled at Jessie to make sure she knew I wasn't worried about being the Temporary Kid. I couldn't tell her the truth . . . that I was more worried about living on the Temporary Planet.

15.
TV Remote Control

The whistle was so shrill it pierced the thick farmhouse walls, and the bedroom door, and the duvet I had pulled over my head. I knew it was Sputnik.

When I slipped downstairs and opened the kitchen door, he was standing there, waiting for me, with his fingers in his mouth, about to whistle again.

– Don't! You'll wake the whole house up.

He tried to push past me into the kitchen.

– You're not supposed to be here. You're supposed to be in Kirkcudbright. What are you doing here?

He took two warm brown eggs out of his sporran and grinned. 'Look at these bad boys. Midnight feast, I think.'

Obviously he wasn't going to fry the eggs himself. That was my job. He curled up on the couch and turned on the telly, only it wasn't tuned in, just a blizzard of hissing interference. 'You know what this is?' asked Sputnik.

– Loud. Very loud.

I rummaged around for the remote.

'That is the sound of background radiation. That is the sound of the beginning of the universe, coming through your telly. It reminds me of the old days when the whole universe was just a little thing the size of a pea. You could pop it in your pocket and cherish it. Then we had that Big Bang nonsense and it kept getting bigger and bigger and now it takes all your strength to get from one side to the other. What are you doing?'

– Pressing the mute button. It's going to wake everyone up. Do you want toast with the egg?

'I thought I'd gone deaf for a minute there, when the sound went. Let me see that. Yes, Sputnik wants toast.'

– We haven't got much time. They're going to send you away in the morning. We've only got tonight to save the world.

'So we need to fuel our brains. I want toast.'

You might think that telling someone he only had one night to save the world would make them listen, but Sputnik just carried on playing with the remote –

whizzing through channels – flicking past cops chasing robbers, robbers chasing cops, someone selling a running machine, a ship sailing through ice. 'I love this. What else does it do?'

– Never mind that now. Think about the list.

But he'd found the pause button and apparently pausing a picture of a woman eating breakfast cereal is hilarious.

– Please. We've got to get thinking.

'This one makes it all go faster, look!' Fast-forwarding someone hoovering a carpet is even more hilarious than pausing a woman mid-breakfast.

I can't even describe how he reacted to the rewind button. I thought he was going to die.

'What else does it work on?'

– Just the telly.

'As if. As if anyone would go to the trouble of making something as brilliant as this just for the telly. Don't touch that egg!'

I had the second egg in my hand. He pointed the remote at it and pressed fast forward. I almost dropped the egg. It shivered in my hand. It cracked at the top. Then there were loads of cracks scribbled all over it. Then one of the cracks lifted like a tiny door and the beak of a chicken pecked out. The chick lifted the top of the shell with the back of its head and looked all around. It was fluffy and yellow as a yolk. It squeaked the highest, weediest cheep I'd ever heard. It really did say, 'Cheep!' just like chicks in picture books. I can't believe I was going to cook it.

'Ha! Brilliant!' Sputnik laughed. Then he pressed rewind and the chick tucked itself back into the egg, pulling the shell after it like a trap door. The scribble of cracks on the shell was erased. Within seconds the egg was whole again. Not a crack. Not a shiver.

'Go on,' said Sputnik. 'Fry it then.'

– I can't fry it now. It's a miracle of fluffy yellow engineering. I've got too much respect to put it in my mouth.

'You told me they had a chicken inside.'

– Yeah, but not a chicken that I've seen. Not a chicken I've heard going *cheep cheep*.

Sputnik was too thrilled with the possibilities of the TV remote to care about the egg. The next thing he pointed it at was the jam jar of tadpoles on the kitchen windowsill.

– No, no, don't! Don't. They're Annabel's.

But he did. There was a little cloud of tadpoles flickering around in water in the jam jar. When

Sputnik pressed fast forward, their tails were sucked into their bodies and little arms and legs sprouted, toes spread, bodies plumped up. Full-grown frogs clambered into the room, plopping on to the carpet. Their croaking sounded like a wet giant belching.

'Whoa! I wasn't expecting that,' whooped Sputnik. 'I thought they'd just swim a bit faster. I never thought they'd change into something else! That's amazing. Does everything round here do that? If I fast forward you, will you turn into a zebra or something?'

He was pointing the remote at me.

– Don't! You're going to wake everyone. You're not even supposed to be here, let alone doing . . . this.

'Stop worrying. All I have to do is press the mute button.' The croaking stopped. It was pretty funny, to be honest, this crowd of frogs squatting on the kitchen rug, their mouths opening and closing but no sound coming out.

'Let's go outside. I want to try rewinding a cow.'

– No, no. It definitely won't work on cows.

But it did.

Frogs on mute is funny, but cows going backwards very fast in the moonlight is completely distracting.

I forgot about everything else and just laughed. I even forgot about the forthcoming destruction of the Earth.

– Shall we put the TV remote on the list?

'Put it down as number one, the star attraction,' whooped Sputnik. Then he shushed me. 'Hush. Hush or I'll mute you. Look.' There was a light moving inside the kitchen. Someone was in there.

Now we're in trouble, I thought.

– Sputnik, go and hide in the shed or something.

But he didn't go and hide in the shed. He went straight back to the house.

– Don't, Sputnik. If they find you . . .

He eased open the kitchen door.

– Don't go in. You've got really muddy feet.

He slipped inside and waved to me to follow him. 'Shush!'

– I'm not actually talking.

But somebody was. Or muttering. And shuffling. With the lights off.

'Torch?' whispered Sputnik as I slid in after him.

– There's one hanging on the back of the door. 'Get it.'

I reached for the torch. Someone hissed, 'What's that noise?'

Someone else answered – very quietly – that they didn't know. 'Just get a move on and we can get out of here.'

Sputnik said, 'Light them up, Prez.'

I turned on the torch, and there they were, squinting into the light, Jez and Ed, the Big Lads from the Hayfield treat. This time they didn't have their little dog with them. What they *did* have was the shortbread tin with all the cash in it.

Jez moved out of the light, looked straight at me and said, 'Shut your mouth.'

No one tells me to shut my mouth.

Because I never open it.

'Jez,' hissed Ed, 'look at the floor.'

I shone the torch at the floor. It seemed like the most polite thing to do. Beady gold frog eyes glittered like a carpet of tiny searchlights. Their mouths opened and closed, closed and opened, but no sound came out of the frogs, or – at first – from the Big Lads.

'What is it?!'

'It's frogs.'

'What's going on with their mouths? Make them stop. It's scaring me.'

'Sure. One touch of a button and . . .' Sputnik

pointed the remote at the frogs, pressed unmute and the room creaked with the croaking of a hundred confused frogs.

'You're going to wake the whole farm. Let's move.'

'How can we? We're surrounded.'

'Just step on them. They're only frogs.'

'I can't. They'll be too squishy.' Ed looked as if he was about to cry.

'We've got the money. Let's go.'

'This,' said Sputnik, jumping up on the couch and cosying down among the cushions, 'is way better than television.'

It *was* pretty funny watching the Big Lads try

to pick their way through the little frogs.

'Are you laughing at me, wee man?'

Maybe I was. I can't remember now. What I can remember is seeing the face of Big Jez pucker with fury. He launched himself across the room at me. He had the tin in his fist. He was going to brain me with it.

I put my hands up to protect my face.

I tried to duck.

I tried to call for help.

Nothing happened.

When I finally got the courage to peep, he was still almost on top of me. But not moving. Not blinking. Not breathing. Still as a statue. No, not like a statue because he seemed to glitter and shimmer like paused pixels. I went to touch him. I thought my hand might go right through him. But . . .

'What've you done to Jez?! What have you done to him?' yelled Ed. He jumped at me too.

Out of the corner of my eye I saw Sputnik's hand go up and he was holding the remote. And then Ed was on pause too. He looked even stranger. He only had one foot on the ground and he was leaning towards me.

– Sputnik! You looked after me! He was going to

hurt me and you stopped him. You finally did look after me!

The paused burglars really were better than television. We sat on the couch and just watched them for about ten minutes. Then we stood for a while, enjoying the frogs hopping over the farmyard cobbles, all heading the same way. Maybe they could smell water or maybe they were just so confused they all just followed the one in front.

I did try and get the money tin out of Jez's hands, but even when he was paused he wasn't going to let go. So we just locked the kitchen door to make sure they didn't escape.

There was a clatter on the stairs.

'More burglars!' whooped Sputnik, spinning round and pointing the remote control. But it wasn't burglars. It was the mum.

'Oh, Sputnik, how did you get back here?! I'll get my coat. We'll have to take him . . .' She stopped. She'd seen the two Big Lads, standing by the door. For a second I thought that Sputnik had freeze-framed her. Then she yelled for help. Jessie, Ray, the dad and even Annabel came running. It all happened so quickly that no one seemed to notice that the two Big Lads were completely still and slightly pixelated. Sputnik pressed play and Big Jez swung the tin of money at where my head had been. Only my head wasn't there any more, so he ended up pirouetting like a bulky ballerina, showering notes and coins all over the kitchen.

'What's he doing?' said Jessie.

'Yeah, what *are* you doing?' said Ed.

Jez stared at the floor, then stared at the Blythes, then stared at me, then pointed. 'Him. He did something to us. What did you do to us?'

I shrugged.

Jessie said, 'The door's locked. Prez must've locked them in.'

'You heard the burglars, didn't you? You came down here and locked them in,' said the dad, looking pleased and puzzled.

'We're not burglars,' said one of the burglars. 'Not really.'

'That was brave, Prez,' said Jessie, looking at the mum and dad.

Everyone applauded me.

Sputnik got up and took a bow.

'And Sputnik of course,' said the mum. 'He came all the way over from Kirkcudbright to protect us from burglars.'

203

'That's what I call a good working farm dog,' said the dad.

'Stop calling us burglars.'

'You were stealing the money from the Hayfield treat! That's for charity. That's worse than burglary.'

'My tadpoles!' shrieked Annabel, pointing to the empty jam jar.

'You stole her tadpoles?!'

'We never did steal her tadpoles. They turned into frogs and attacked us.'

'My tadpoles!' sobbed Annabel.

'How could you steal a little girl's tadpoles?' snapped the mum.

'We DIDN'T STEAL THEM.'

'Don't shout at my wife, son,' said the dad.

'How could a dog do all that?' sniffed Ed.

'He's not even a dog,' muttered Jez.

'Frogs!' Ed was completely sobbing now. 'Hundreds of frogs.'

The dad made them pick up all the money and count it. It was daylight by then. Then the dad went outside and had a long chat with someone on the phone. When he came back in, he was telling whoever it was to come over as soon as possible.

Jez and Ed sat on the couch, as silent as if they'd been muted. They knew they were going to be taken away. I couldn't help but think about Grandad and wonder if he felt this bad when he found out they were going to take him away.

A car pulled up, but it wasn't the police. The dad had rung the priest instead. When he arrived, the dad made Jez and Ed hand the money over to him. The priest didn't know about the burglary. He just kept telling them what a great job they'd done and what grand lads they were, until Ed squealed, 'We're not, Father. We tried to steal the money but we're sorry now.'

After breakfast Mrs Rowland from the Temporary came round.

'Well, Prez,' she said, 'you'll be pleased to hear that your grandad is finally accepting his new environment.' I pictured Grandad in a prison uniform, queuing up for prison food with a prison haircut. 'As soon as he's properly settled, I'll take you over for a visit, maybe at the end of next week just before you go back to school.'

I didn't say anything. I wanted to see him. But I didn't want to see him in jail.

'And the dog? You did get rid of the dog?'

'We had a think about that,' said the dad, looking around the room. Almost invisibly everyone nodded at him, as if he'd asked them a silent question, as if they could all read each other's thoughts the way that Sputnik could read mine.

'Oh?' said Mrs Rowland.

'I asked around a bit and it turns out that the fierce dog isn't Sputnik.'

'It isn't your dog?'

'No. I asked Dmitri in the shop to describe the dog that attacked him. I'll call him and put him on speakerphone so you can hear . . .'

The dad rang Dmitri. Sputnik strolled in and sat down with his head on one side, smiling up at Mrs Rowland.

Dmitri answered the phone. He said he was very happy to describe the dog that attacked him. It was 'a big beastie, a bit like a Dobermann but uncommon huge with deep empty eyes and – I know this sounds strange – there was smoke coming out of his ears.'

'Is that man talking about me?' whimpered Sputnik. 'So. Rude.'

'Seems to be a case –' the dad shrugged – 'of mistaken dog identity.'

'Yes,' said Mrs Rowland. 'He's nothing like a Dobermann. More like a Labrador.'

'I thought lurcher cross,' said the dad. 'But either way, we'll be keeping Sputnik and he'll be welcome in the house any time.'

So Sputnik had a new home, a permanent one. But we were running out of time to save the world. The summer would be over and the leaves would begin to fall, and that, as Sputnik had made clear, would be that.

16.
Curtains

Now that he didn't have to sneak in, Sputnik explored the whole house. He found the entire place fascinating. He took photos. He took notes. He unpacked all his stuff – spare kilt, spare sporran. He emptied his backpack out on the top bunk in Ray's room.

'Aren't you going to unpack your backpack?' he asked.

– No point. I'm going back to the Temporary soon.

This didn't seem to bother him. He nibbled the curtains.

– Curtains are not edible.

'They've got fruit on them, look. Blackberries, raspberries.'

– They're just pictures.

'Yes. Pictures. Of fruit. Why would anyone

put a picture of something edible on something inedible?

– They just look nice.

'They look tasty. But they're not tasty. They are curtains of lies and disappointment. They are not going in the *Companion*.'

And he finally got stuck into finishing his list. He piled up history books and atlases. He printed out train timetables, star maps and stuff about bird migration. He stuck his list-so-far up on the ceiling over the top bunk so we could discuss it in detail and save the world together.

TV Remote
High-Vis Jackets
The Atmosphere
The Tide
Chickens and Eggs
Prez's Grandad's Harmonica
Concealer
Mooring Hitch Knot

– Hitch knots? Really?

'Definitely. That hammock was the best night's sleep I've ever had, like lying on a big antigravity mattress. We are well on the way to saving your planet. Got any other ideas?'

– I can't think of a single thing worth doing or seeing.

'There must be something.'

– What's it like on *your* planet? What things are worth seeing there?

'I told you. I don't have a planet. Planetary Clearance got to it years ago. I wander round the universe like a comet.'

– But where do you live?

'I live where I am.'

– But you must have something. Like a rocket?

'Rocket? Where are you from, the Stone Age? No one uses rockets any more.'

– So how do you travel through space?

'I don't know. Just a kind of knack. It's not like space is flat. It's rippled and curved. And it moves about. It's alive. You learn to ride it after a while.'

– But you can't travel faster than light. Nothing can.

'No. But you can take a shortcut. However far you go, you always end up where you started. Except for the gloves obviously.'

– The gloves? What gloves? Why?

'The thing about the universe is it's bent. I'll show you.' He took a strip of paper, gave it a twist, then held the ends together. 'You think it's got two sides, don't you? But run your finger along it.'

I traced my finger along the paper.

– It's just got one side.

'It's called a Möbius strip. That's what the universe is like. If you set off in a straight line, you end up where you started. Except that you're the other way round. If you've got a left-hand glove, it's on your right hand. You become your own reflection.'

I tried it again the other way round.

– So you don't live on a rocket. You don't live on a planet. Where *do* you live?

'The Centre of the Universe. That's my address.'

– Where's that?

'Well, where's the centre of infinity? Think about it. The centre of infinity is everywhere. From wherever you're standing, infinity stretches out infinitely in every direction. It's infinite that way. And that way. And that way. Therefore you must be in the middle. Wherever you are, that's the centre of the universe.'

– But don't you have a home?

'Of course I do! Every port I land at, every safe harbour is home. For a while. Come on. All hands on deck. Let's steer this planet through the storm and save it from extinction. Think of something worth seeing or doing. Keep trying. We don't have forever. Well, we do, but forever isn't very long.'

I'm trying but I can't think of anything except Grandad in jail. Sitting in a cell. Or queuing for food. All because he got mixed up about chopping vegetables.

– The world's not fair. Maybe it's not worth saving.

I pulled the duvet over my head.

I don't know how long I was lying there like that before I had the idea.

Of course there was something on Earth I wanted to see. And of course I could go and see it.

I woke Sputnik.

– I've thought of something.

'Shush. You'll wake Ray. It's the middle of the night.'

– I know, but I've thought of something.

Something really worth seeing. You'll love it.

'If you can't get to sleep, turn around three times and then lie down really quickly.'

– No, no. It's better that it's night-time.

'What is it? What are we going to see?'

– My grandad.

'But your grandad's in jail.'

– Yes. But I've got a plan.

'A plan?' said Sputnik, sitting up in bed. 'I love a plan. What is it?'

– A jailbreak.

'A jailbreak?' Sputnik hitched up his kilt. Fastened his flying helmet. Pulled down his goggles.

'I'm in,' he said.

We slipped downstairs. Sputnik whispered, 'So how are we going to do this?'

– I thought we could bring the remote and you could put all the guards on pause while we got him out.

We looked everywhere for the remote – down the back of the couch, under the television. We couldn't find it anywhere. Why do remotes always go missing just when you want them?

'What about the lightsaber? We could cut

213

through bars and fences with that.'

– The batteries are gone. Someone must have borrowed them for the remote.

'Never mind,' said Sputnik. 'Let's go. We'll think of something.'

I took my phone, and as we crossed the farmyard I dived into the tractor shed and grabbed a torch and some wire cutters.

The 63 is a late bus that runs along the main road into Dumfries. Everyone calls it the booze bus because it stops at all the pubs it passes. We got on

it just outside Dmitri's shop. When it stopped at Whitesands, the driver got out, locked the bus and went home.

– Perfect. We need a getaway vehicle. What could be more inconspicuous than a bus?

'Can you drive a bus?'

– We don't need to drive it. Once we've got Grandad, we'll get back on board and hide on it until morning. Then when it heads back to Kirkcudbright, we get off at the loaning, walk down to the farm and hide Grandad in the Coo Palace. We can feed him and keep him company and he can get washed at the sinks. It's even got a toilet. He can live like a king in a castle until the police forget about him.

'That sounds like a plan,' said Sputnik.

But things don't always go according to plan.

17.
Jailbreak

The prison didn't look like I thought it would.

It was on an ordinary street with no barbed-wire fence or guards.

So some of the plans I had – such as cutting through the barbed wire with the wire cutters I had borrowed from the big barn, or tying up the guards with the twine from the hay-baler – weren't really that useful.

– We could dig a tunnel.

'Have you brought a spade?'

– No, but . . .

'I'm not digging a tunnel. I'm not a dog. I'm the Sputnik. I go in through the front door.'

Which is exactly what he did.

There was a door marked 'Reception'. He opened it and strolled in. Inside there was one of those hatches with a window and a thing to talk through.

Behind the glass was a big hefty bloke in a white shirt, watching a CCTV monitor and slurping a purple Slush Puppie.

'I'm Sputnik Mellows,' said Sputnik. 'I'm here to do a jailbreak. Just try and stop me, Big Hefty Bloke in a White Shirt.'

Big Hefty Bloke put down the Slush Puppie, pushed back his window and looked at Sputnik. 'Hello,' he said. 'Aren't you cheeky?' Then he looked at me.

'What is he?'

'Errrm . . . mostly terrier,' I said. 'Whistling terrier.'

'Good work,' said Sputnik. 'You keep him talking. I'll go and jailbreak your grandad.' There was a serious-looking metal door in front of us. Sputnik was sizing it up.

I said, 'You can't just stroll in and jailbreak someone. You have to have a plan of action. Disguises. Gadgets. Alibis. You don't even know what my grandad looks like. Never mind what cell he's in!'

Big Hefty Bloke was staring at me. That's when I realized.

'I said that out loud, didn't I?' It must have been

because I was thinking I was going to see Grandad any minute.

'So you're going to do a jailbreak?' asked the man.

'Going to jailbreak his grandad,' said Sputnik. 'I know exactly what he looks like because the boy has a photo of him in his backpack, which he looks at every time he gets his pyjamas out.'

Obviously Big Hefty Bloke didn't understand any of that. He was still staring at me.

I said, 'Jailbreak. Yeah. Why not?' There didn't seem much point denying it.

'So what is your plan? Knock me on the head, disguise yourself in my uniform and steal my keys?'

'It worked in Colditz,' I said. 'Twice.' I had been researching jailbreaks on my phone all the way on the bus.

'My clothes might be a bit big for you – by about twenty sizes. Plus I don't have keys. We're all electronic now. I thought they built a glider in Colditz?'

'They did, but it took so long the war was over by the time they finished it.'

'So you haven't got a glider?'

'Not yet. You can check if you like.' I held my hands up as though I might have a glider tucked away in my trousers.

He laughed and took another slurp of Slush Puppie. Which is probably why he never saw – on his CCTV – Sputnik moving quickly and quietly along the corridors of the prison.

'Then there's Bonnie Prince Charlie,' I said. 'He got out of jail by disguising himself as a woman and sneaking out that way.'

'As this is an all-male facility,' said Big Hefty bloke, 'I don't think being disguised as a woman is going to help. It's only going to make you more conspicuous.' He seemed happy to spend time giving me lots of jailbreak advice. I think he probably thought I wasn't serious. When he said, 'Why not dig a tunnel?' for instance, he was definitely using a shouldn't-you-be-at-home-in-bed voice.

'I thought about it. Takes too long and my accomplice doesn't really like digging.'

'Mass breakout? All guns blazing?'

'I hate guns.'

'Very wise. John Dillinger . . .'

'He used a gun but it was a fake gun made out of soap and boot polish. That was good. But my grandad doesn't know I'm jailbreaking him. It's sort of a surprise.'

'Helicopter? A helicopter is always a treat.'

'Haven't got one.'

I was actually enjoying talking.

'Ladder over the wall?'

'My grandad's not so steady on his feet.'

'Smuggled out in the laundry basket?'

'Do you have laundry baskets?'

'Not really.'

'All the best jailbreaks are when someone just strolls out the front door.'

'That's true. Though of course, in this case, they'd have to get past me. And not much gets past me.'

As he was saying this, I could see Sputnik on the CCTV monitor, looking straight into camera and giving me a thumbs-up. Then all the monitor screens flickered and died. 'What now?' Big Hefty Bloke sighed. He went to fiddle with the console, but as he turned away from me there was a whirring sound and a metal screen began to unroll across the window of his hatch. 'What's going on? This is the emergency failsafe.' He tried to block the metal roller with his hand but it just kept coming. 'Ow!' he yelped, snatching his hand away and sucking his finger. He dashed to his office door, trying to get through to my side, but I heard a loud metal click.

'What's happening?' he yelled.

'I told you . . . we're jailbreaking my grandad.'

The lights went out.

All of them.

Sputnik had closed down the entire electronic security system.

On the other side of the metal screen I could hear Big Hefty Bloke desperately pressing buttons on his phone. I could hear a recorded voice replying, 'The number you have dialled has not been recognized. Please check and try again.'

Then the serious-looking metal door clicked open.

The only light came from one of those blue lamps that are supposed to kill flies. I could see the glint of Sputnik's goggles bouncing towards me and a crowd of big, uncertain shadows following him.

'I couldn't figure out which one was your grandad,' he said, 'so I brought them all.'

'You brought me a busload of criminals?'

'Your grandad's a criminal. What better place to hide him than among a busload of criminals? Come on – to the 63 bus stop at Whitesands.'

*

Sputnik had killed the street lights too. The whole town was in darkness. We could hear the water roaring over the weir. Moonlight brightened the windows of the waiting bus, as though the moon was helping us find our getaway vehicle. The 63 has sliding doors, the kind with a rubber seal. If you can squeeze something into the gap, it's easy to force the doors open. I used my backpack to keep them open.

The prisoners seemed to know that they'd better not cause a stramash. The quiet shadows of the escaped prisoners piled on to the bus. I tried to look into their faces as they passed but they were looking down. I poked around in the driver's cab with my torch until I found the switch; then I put the lights on.

'Grandad?' I called out excitedly. 'It's me. Prez!'

First one head, then another, then another popped up from behind the seats where they had been hiding.

Some were big.

Some were small.

Some were fat.

Some thin. Some white. One black.

One had a big scar right down the middle of his head.

They looked like stubble-headed meerkats watching out for police hyenas.

None of them looked even a little bit like Grandad.

'Grandad . . . ?' I asked. 'Is my grandad . . . Sandy Mellows . . . is he here?'

A small one with narrow eyes and hardly any teeth when he grinned said, 'You're looking for your grandad?'

'Yeah.'

'And you thought he was in Nithsdale with us lot?'

'Yeah, I thought so.'

'How old's your grandad?'

'I don't know. Normal age. Normal age for a grandad.'

'You've just helped us escape from Nithsdale

Young Offenders Institution. Maximum age eighteen. Is your grandad under eighteen?'

'I don't think so.'

'If you haven't got a teenage grandad . . .'

'I've made a mistake.'

'It looks that way.' The one with the scar on his head started laughing. The others joined in. 'Thanks all the same by the way.'

I said, 'I'm really sorry about the mix-up. I'm going to have to take you back. Sputnik will help you get back in.'

'Oh,' said Hardly Any Teeth, 'you'll help us get back in jail? Well, that's very kind of you. Thanks a million. Did you hear that, Smash? He's going to put us back in prison.'

Unsurprisingly Smash turned out to be the one with the scar down the middle of his forehead. He looked me up and down and said, 'Well, boys, what do we say to the wee man's kind offer?'

What they said was:

HA HA HA HA
HA HA HA HA HA HA HA HA HA HA HA HA HA HA HA HA
HA HA HA HA HA HA HA HA HA HA HA HA HA HA HA HA
HA HA HA HA HA HA HA HA HA HA HA HA HA HA HA HA.

They laughed until the bus rocked.

'Err, no,' said Hardly Any Teeth, 'we're no going back. Not for you. Not for anyone. We're taking this bus and we're going to faraway Carlisle. I've got cousins there.'

'No, not Carlisle. We're away to Glasgow. It'll be easier to get lost there.'

'Is Newcastle not nearer? I like Newcastle. We went with school one time.'

'What about the kid?'

'I live near Knockbrex.'

'Nothing is near Knockbrex.'

'He's coming with us. We'll take him hostage. You don't mind if we take you hostage, do you, kid?'

'What about heading over to Stranraer? No one goes there.'

'Stranraer is always buzzing with police. For the ferries.'

While they were discussing where to go, the bus started up and moved off. It skidded across the tarmac, scraped through the metal barriers and swung on to the road.

'Just a minute,' said Smash. 'Who's driving this bus?'

'Me!' yelled Sputnik. He leaned out from the

driver's cab and waved at everyone. The bus shuddered. He'd bounced off a lamp post. 'Whoops!' said Sputnik.

There was one of those short silences that feel really long – like when you drop a pebble down a deep, deep drain. Even though you can't hear a noise yet, you know that there is going to be a noise.

Then the noise comes.

A scream. Smash screamed first. 'There's a dog. There's a dog and it's driving the bus.'

The Chubby One knelt down in the gangway and started saying his prayers very, very loud.

Hardly Any Teeth just got right in my face and kept yelling, 'Stop! Now! Make it stop!'

– I think they're upset that you're driving the bus.

'I haven't hit anything. Much. Nothing important anyway. I haven't crashed. Why the fuss?! Don't they trust me?'

– It just feels wrong – a dog driving a bus.

'Explain that I'm not a dog.'

– Couldn't you just show them that you're not a dog?

'If driving a bus brilliantly – which is what I'm doing – doesn't convince them that I'm not a dog, what will? Shall I drive faster?'

226

– No! Don't drive faster.

But he did drive faster.

And faster.

Up on to the bypass, around a traffic island. Prisoners tumbled into the gangway like skittles.

– Stop. Stop the bus.

He swerved on to the exit for the twenty-four-hour Tesco. He slammed through the shrubs and over a few signs. He parked the bus in the thing that you're supposed to park your shopping trolley in. The bus didn't really fit, to be honest.

The prisoners were all crouching at the back by now.

'Why are you doing these terrible things to us?' screamed the really big one. 'We didn't do anything to you.'

Smash was banging on the window, shouting, 'Help! Help!'

The Chubby One was shouting, 'Call the police! I want to go back to jail. I only came to look after the little doggy. I thought the little doggy was lost.'

I went to the driver's seat and blew into the driver's microphone. It sounded like a mighty wind. Then I spoke. I was starting to enjoy speaking, especially amplified speaking. 'Stop making a noise.

You're attracting attention.'

'Attracting attention?! Your dog just drove a BUS the wrong way up the bypass.'

'Oh.'

– Did you drive the wrong way?

'I drove it the way we need to go – west.'

– Yeah, but what side of the road?

He didn't answer. He just started up the engine again. Which started up the prisoners screaming again.

'Let us off!'

'Let us off the bus!'

'I saw the wee mutt and thought he was lost. All I wanted to do was help the little doggy.'

'And all I wanted to do was find my grandad.' I sighed and sat down.

'Solero,' said Hardly Any Teeth. I followed his gaze. His face was pressed up against the window. He was staring at a big lit-up Solero advert in the entrance to the Tesco. The orange lolly in the picture glowed with flavour. In the photograph, it was just beginning to melt. That Solero was one long, hot summer day on a stick. The others all joined him at the window, staring out at the Tesco car park.

'Trolleys,' said the one with the scar in his head. 'Did anyone ever race shopping trolleys down Heathall Rise?'

'That sounds dangerous,' said Hardly Any Teeth.

'A wee bit,' agreed Smash. 'When I first started trolley racing my nickname was Dash. Then I got a wee bit reckless and' – he pointed to his head – 'Smash.'

'Look at all these cars,' said Hardly Any Teeth. 'I used to love "borrowing" cars and driving them round the bypass. I haven't done that since . . . well . . . since they caught me.'

'There's a chip van, look. Does it do hot dogs?'

'Couldn't we just have one treat? Like some Cool Original Doritos. Do we really have to go straight back?' said the Chubby One.

'Or Chilli Heatwave.'

'OK, this is what we'll do,' said Hardly Any Teeth. 'You go and get us some treats, bring them out here and then we'll decide where we're going to go.'

I said, 'I can't just get you a load of treats. I've got no money.'

'Not our problem.'

'How am I going to pay for this?'

'Shoplift.'

'Do not shoplift. You don't want to end up like us.'

'How can I do it without money and without stealing?'

'That's your problem,' said Hardly Any Teeth. 'Get us some beer too. A pie and a pint or a hostage situation. You decide.'

Sputnik had never been inside a supermarket before. 'And to think I thought Dmitri's shop had loads of stuff,' he gasped, staring at the racks of vegetables – the glossy peppers, the plump apples, the glowing lemons. He stared at the cool aisle – the hunks of cheese, the slabs of meat, the piles of butter, the bottles of juice. He stared at the signs swinging over the aisles – Pasta, Cook-In Sauces, Dairy, Biscuits, Crisps, Cereal . . . 'Everything . . .' he sighed. 'Everything in here is so' – he searched for the word – 'edible.'

– Yeah, but you can't eat it until you've paid for it.

'Everything is so, so tasty.'

– And we don't have any money.

'I can sidestep that problem,' said Sputnik, opening his backpack.

– No. No guns. Absolutely no guns.

I looked around. There was hardly anyone in the store. A couple of people in nurse's uniform were chatting by the sandwiches. Someone was restocking the baked-bean shelves. No one said anything when Sputnik flew down the bread aisle, on the back of a trolley, and swung left into Beers and Wine.

– I said, I'm not allowed to buy beer. You've got to be over eighteen.

'I am over eighteen. I'm over 18 million,' said Sputnik, sweeping two bottles of Criffel Ale into the trolley and rolling on into Crisps and Treats (aisle 7). He shovelled Doritos and Pringles and Irn-Bru in with the beer as he headed for the checkout.

– The checkouts don't work if you're under age. Also you have to put money in them.

'Your attitude is all wrong. You see the checkout as your enemy. Like it wants to stop you having fun. The checkout wants you to have a nice time and get nice things.'

– No. It wants me to pay.

'Have you read the manual?' asked Sputnik.

– No. Because I'm a customer, not a checkout person.

'Ever tried to speak to the checkout in its own language?'

– It speaks English.

'It speaks,' said Sputnik, pulling his little torch out of his backpack, 'binary. Look. See the stripes on the bar code? They make little dots and dashes of light. That's the language it likes to talk. There're thousands of languages on this planet. You should learn some.' He pointed the torch straight at the scanner and flashed it on and off and off and on, quickly then slowly, like a code.

The self-checkout beeped and re-beeped, then beeped again.

'See?' said Sputnik. 'It's giggling. It likes me. It's been lonely, poor thing.' He flickered the light on and off a few more times. The self-checkout beeped again, then said, 'Change will be dispensed below the reader.'

– But we can't get any change – we haven't put any money in.

'I just adjusted the sequence. Normally you pay for stuff and it gives change. Now it's going to give change and *then* we'll pay for stuff.'

– I think you've missed the whole point of 'change'. In a completely illegal way.

'Honestly,' said the self–checkout, 'I have *much* more money than I could ever spend.'

A ten-pound note slid out of its dispenser. Then another. And another. Then a fistful of change rattled into the tray like when you win on an arcade game.

No one seemed to have noticed. I turned to the trolley to get the beers and crisps. There was other stuff in there – pasta, cherry tomatoes, onions, a chilli, oregano, some cheese and a bottle of Worcester sauce.

– What's all this?

'You know what it is. Ingredients for your grandad's favourite quick tea. Pasta with a fresh tomato sauce and a bit of fresh chilli.'

I could smell the oregano and the chilli. It was like Grandad was back in the room.

– How did you know that?

'I can read your thoughts. Even the ones you don't know you're thinking.'

– What's the point in buying Grandad's favourite ingredients when I don't even know where he is?

'You'll find him. Trust Sputnik.'

– Trust Sputnik. Trust the Sputnik who said he would look after me, the Sputnik who put me on a bus with a load of convicted criminals, driven by a dog.

'I'm not a dog.'

– You drive like a dog.

I scanned all the tomatoes and pasta and stuff. Then I tried to scan a bottle of beer.

'Assistance required,' said the self-checkout. Its number light flashed. A supervisor came over. She looked at the beer. She looked at me.

'I'm afraid I'll have to ask you for ID,' she said. 'You don't look over eighteen.' This was not surprising.

I did think of going to get one of the prisoners to buy their own beer, but then I thought, Do I really want people to know that the busload of escaped convicts in the car park belongs to me?

'I don't have ID.'

'Then you can't buy the beer.'

'Oh,' whined the self-checkout, 'go on.'

The supervisor blinked, then stared at the machine.

'Go on,' repeated the self-checkout. 'Just this once.'

'Errrm,' said the supervisor, 'is this some kind of

prank? Is it for training purposes?'

'Yes. This is for training purposes,' said the self-checkout.

'I can't let him buy beer without ID.'

'Please comply with request,' said the checkout.

The supervisor looked nervous.

'Your compliance is required,' insisted the checkout. It was beginning to sound like a short-tempered Dalek. The supervisor looked frightened.

'Comply.'

'OK, OK, I'll comply!'

When I got outside, the prisoners were all sitting on the railings by the trolley shelter, waiting. They gave a big cheer when they saw us coming and put out their hands for the treats.

'I used to come down here when I was a wean,' said Hardly Any Teeth, crowding a fistful of Pringles into his mouth. 'Whenever there was no one home, I came down here.'

'Me too! How brilliant is that?!' said Smash. 'I used to come down here and skateboard.'

'We used to lob bottles at the skateboarders,' said Hardly Any Teeth, sucking on his Solero now.

'And we used to lob the bottles back.'

'So we probably used to throw bottles at each other! Coincidence or what?'

'Amazing.'

They made it sound like throwing bottles at each other was a bit like being long-lost cousins. They tucked into Doritos and Pringles. They guzzled Irn-Bru.

'It wasn't open all night back in the day,' said the Chubby One. 'I used to daydream about living in the store.'

'So did I!' said Hardly Any Teeth.

'I used to imagine myself under a pile of duvets in the bedding department. And getting up early before anyone came in and grabbing myself a bowl from household goods, a carton of milk from dairy, then just going up and down the cereals aisle, taking whatever I wanted.'

'I was mostly thinking about hanging around in the frozen section munching Arctic rolls and Magnums.'

Irn-Bru, Magnums, Arctic rolls – I was beginning to realize that the boys had no idea about nutrition. I went over to the van and bought us all fish and chips with the money that the self-checkout had given me. We sat on a wall by the garage forecourt and ate them.

'Hot food outdoors,' said Sputnik. 'This is the best thing ever.'

'I did live here for a bit,' said Smash. 'Not inside – security was too tight – but there was a heating pipe round the back that was always nice and warm and there were plenty of cardboard boxes to make a bed, I used to do that when things were bad at home. Or that time I ran away from the Temporary.'

'You were in the Temporary?' I asked.

'Yeah,' said Smash. 'Four years. I didn't like it, but then I left and I had nowhere at all so the Temporary seemed like Shangri-La.'

'Shangri-La?'

Before I could ask anything else, he said, 'Let's have a trolley race.'

They raced the trolleys around the car park until Security came out and chased them back on to the bus.

They argued about who was going to sit where while I hung back in the doorway, holding my bag of shopping. They squirted Irn-Bru at each other. Hardly Any Teeth blew into his Doritos bag, then popped it like a balloon. All the others laughed and copied him. I wasn't scared of them any more. They weren't convicts. They were just boys who didn't have homes to go to.

'Come in,' yelled Hardly Any Teeth. 'Let's go!'

'Go where?' I said.

'The Young Offenders'.' Smash shrugged. 'We've got nowhere else to go.'

Sputnik tried to jump into the driver's seat. 'Oh no,' said Hardly Any Teeth, 'we're not being driven by a dog. I'm in for joyriding. I might as well use my skills to get us home.'

So he drove the bus back along the bypass and up to the doors of the Young Offenders'. I've got to admit he was a much better driver than Sputnik.

The sun was coming up as they filed in through reception. Sputnik reset the security system. The metal roller blind came up. Big Hefty Bloke was sitting behind it, his eyes wide as though he'd never seen daylight before. He stared at the obedient prisoners on his CCTV. Some of them waved at the camera.

'What happened?' said the Big Hefty Bloke.

'Sorry,' I said. I handed him a purple Slush Puppie. 'I got you this to make up for it.'

*

We got the bus back to the bus stop just in time for its first trip of the day. We sat at the back while the driver drove us down through Dalbeattie.

'You didn't get your grandad,' said Sputnik.

– No.

'At least I got something for the list.'

– What was that? Supermarkets? Self-checkouts?

'Chips. Who invented them?'

– No one. I think they just sort of happened.

'Just sort of happened? What, everyone in the world thought, What if we dig that plant over there up by its big knobbly roots, and peel the skin off the roots and then cut the roots into thin strips, and then what if we get some fat from a cow and melt that down and make it boiling hot, and drop the strips of potato in the boiling fat? And then . . . why don't we get some grapes and crush them and wait till the juice has gone sour and pour that over the fried potatoes? And then—'

– OK. I get it. Chips are complicated. No one invented them. Everyone invented them. Bit by bit. Over a long time.

'Well, that's something I love about your species. How everyone helps to make an idea better and better until after about a hundred years it's completely brilliant. Fish and chips are like a big knot tying everyone together. We can put that on the list. Fish and chips outside can go in the *Companion*.'

– OK.

There was no one on the bus but us. The fields were empty. I wondered where everyone was. No, I didn't. I just wondered where Grandad was.

18.
Geese

It wasn't just Grandad who was missing. When we got back to Stramoddie, there was no car in the farmyard. The front door was open, but there was no one in the house. We ran up to the pasture. The cows were out, but there was no one there. The Coo Palace was deserted. I shouted everyone's names but the only answer was the hens all running round being stressed. No one had collected their eggs. I carried them into the kitchen and put them in a bowl next to my shopping.

– Aren't you worried that everyone's gone missing?

'Not really. I think we could manage here fine on our own. Plenty of cows to eat.'

I was scared that something terrible had happened. That something even more terrible might happen. I took Grandad's chopping knife out of my backpack and put it in my pocket.

As if they'd heard what Sputnik had said, the cows started mooing. I ran to the window. The Blythes' car was rolling down the loaning. I opened the front door.

'There he is!'

'We were so worried about you!'

'I wasn't worried. I knew you'd just gone off for a walk together.'

'I said he probably just didn't want to go to Mass.'

They'd been at church. I'd forgotten it was Sunday.

I took Grandad's chopping knife out of my pocket and held it in my hand. The mum looked at it.

Then she smiled and said, 'Are you going to help me cook?'

Then the dad spotted the Tesco bag. 'He's been shopping. Are you going to cook for us?'

All I knew was I wanted to peel and chop things. I wanted to do something that my grandad could do. Something that would make me feel like he hadn't vanished off the face of the Earth.

In the kitchen, the mum showed me a chicken.

'It's the brown one. The one that hardly ever laid but made loads of noise.'

'She didn't kill her for lunch,' said Ray. 'She killed her for revenge.'

'But we can still eat her for lunch.'

The dad showed me how to do roast potatoes, because I'd never done them. Then I did the tomato and chilli sauce. It didn't really go with the roast chicken, but the smell of the chilli, and the way the tomatoes went sticky if you grated them and cooked them really slowly, was exactly how Grandad did it.

After we'd eaten I helped move the cows into the Coo Palace for milking. Sputnik went up the tower while we were fixing the pumps. He shouted, 'Come and look at this!'

'What's he making such a racket about?' said the dad, heading off up the stairs to investigate. 'I sometimes get the impression Sputnik is trying to tell us something.'

'I'm trying to tell you,' said Sputnik, 'that the sky is full of food!'

Geese.

At first they were just dark smudges on the sky out over the sea. Then you could see that the smudges were dots. Then *V*-shapes. Then all at once they

were overhead, honking like ships' foghorns, their
big wings hauling their fat bellies through the air.
Wave after wave of them came. It felt as if it would
go on forever. They flew so low over our heads that
sometimes we had to duck down. They landed on
the Merse and on the fields around the caravan site.
And when they landed they were noisier than ever,
stretching their necks and blasting the sky with their
honks.

'They've been in Iceland all summer,' said the
dad. He had to shout over the noise of them. 'They
come back every year in autumn. Same fields.
The honking is the wives and husbands trying to
find each other. They're moving into their winter
homes. It's amazing. They come all the way from

Iceland to the same field every year. Eight hundred miles. They never get lost. But they also never warn the others that people shoot them and eat them. I suppose home is home, even if people are shooting at you.'

'Can we shoot at them?' said Sputnik.

– No.

That was the end of my stay.

Next morning I went back to the Temporary.

19.
Be Nice

I didn't have to pack (because I kept everything in my backpack).

I didn't have to say goodbye. ('We'll not say goodbye,' the mum said, 'because you're welcome here any time.')

I didn't have to worry. ('Don't worry about Sputnik,' said Jessie. 'I'll look after him').

('Don't worry about me,' said Sputnik. 'I'll be out of here and on my way home first thing in the morning.')

– But it can't be over just like that.

'Honestly. I'll be fine. Stop worrying about me.'

– I'm not worrying about *you*. I'm worrying about me. And my grandad. And the planet.

'Finished my list. Mission accomplished. Thank you and goodbye.' Sputnik tugged on the straps of his backpack.

– What? You've got ten things?! You never told me.

He waved his red notebook. 'It's all in here,' he said.

– Show me.

'OK, I've got nine things right now, but I'll find the last one easily. There's loads of things worth seeing on this planet. I don't need your help.'

But I needed his help. I needed him to help me find Grandad. I knew he wouldn't help me unless I tricked him into it. So I had to think without him hearing me. It wasn't easy. I had to put one big loud thought at the front of my brain and have a quiet little shifty think in the back of my mind. It was a bit like that thing where you swing your left arm forwards and your right arm backwards. At the front of my brain I thought:

– BUT YOU HAVEN'T FINISHED YOUR LIST.

'Yes, I have. Well, nearly.' He started to reel off his list: 'Earth's atmosphere, eggs, the television remote . . .'

– The TV remote is rubbish.

'What?! It was brilliant. I foiled a robbery with it. I could have done a jailbreak with it if we could have found it in time . . .'

– Exactly. That's the thing about TV remotes. Whenever you want them, you can't find them. It's a design flaw. TV remotes are just very, very losable.

'I'll fix that. I bet if you read the manual . . .'

– I've got something better.

'What?'

– Something really amazing.

'What?' I could feel him poking around in my mind to see if I really did have something wonderful to show him.

– That's cheating.

It felt like lemonade spilling inside my head. I was trying to put something exciting in there, but I couldn't think of one thing I wanted to see on the whole planet. Apart from my grandad. And he had disappeared.

'I can't see anything exciting inside your head,' said Sputnik. 'Plus I'm suspicious of your motives.'

He was right to be suspicious of my motives. I needed to trick him into finding Grandad.

How do you lie to someone who can read your mind?

In my imagination I pictured Grandad's sea chest. I added a few fancy bolts and locks and nice bits of metalwork to it. I knew Sputnik could see it somehow. Then I thought . . .

– Remember this? Grandad's sea chest back at the flat? No one knows what's inside. Only my grandad has the keys.

'I don't need keys. I can shoot the lock off.'

– But maybe what's inside is

something delicate and fragile. Maybe it's got a curse on it. No, you definitely need to find my grandad if you're ever going to solve the secret of the sea chest.

'It's probably just jewels or something. Doesn't interest me. There's an entire moon made of diamond a few doors up from the Crab Nebula. There's an asteroid made of ruby that I sometimes hitch a ride on. Honestly, treasure is dull.'

– I think it might be something to do with Shangri-La.

'Shangri-La is a mythical kingdom in the Himalayas where no one ever gets old or ill.'

– I know. I've been there. Look. It's on my map.

'You've been to a mythical kingdom?'

– I don't remember much about it.

'You've been to a mythical magical kingdom where no one ever gets old or ill, but you don't remember much about it?'

– It's on my map, look. I could take you back there. Come on – it's got to be better than a TV remote.

'I'll think it over.'

Mrs Rowland's car came down the loaning. She thanked everyone. I climbed in and that was that.

'Let me get a sniff of you,' said Sputnik. 'That way if I do need you, I can come and find you.'

'Sputnik's crying!' said the mum, misinterpreting his sniffing. 'He's sad to see you go.'

'Don't be sad, Sputnik,' said Ray.

'He wants to go with Prez,' said Jessie.

'You don't want to live in the town, Sputnik,' said the dad. 'You want to stay here where there's grass and space. And work to do.'

'We're going to have a great time here. Aren't we?' said Ray, ruffling Sputnik's hair.

'If he doesn't stop ruffling my hair, I'm going

to shoot him,' said Sputnik.

  — It's horrible when you talk about people in front of them like that. Just because you know they can't understand you. He really likes you.

  'He thinks I'm a dog.'

  — He likes dogs.

  'It's not about how I look. It's about how they see. You see different.'

  — Be nice to them.

The car drove off. I looked back at them all waving.

  'Sounds like you've had a very nice summer,' said Mrs Rowland, 'and made a very good impression. Well done, Prez.'

  On the drive back I thought that if I started talking she might think I'd done so well that I should go back and stay there. I thought of a few things to say, but before I could put a sentence together we were there. Mrs Rowland's car is a lot quicker than the number 63 bus.

20.
Spaghetti

It was strange being back at the Temporary, strange to wake up to the sound of buses and milkmen instead of chickens and cows. There were some new kids, and a few of the old kids had left but – apart from the faces – everything was just the same. Murder Bell was still there. Dinner was still spaghetti Bolognese with a sauce that came out of a jar. I mean, why do that? It must be cheaper to chop up a few tomatoes and onions. A new kid with spiky hair cut his spaghetti into little pieces before eating it. Where's the fun in that? Murder laughed when he heard I'd spent the whole summer in Stramoddie. He said his family had taken him to Florida. This turned out not to be true.

21.
Fire Drill

I woke up in the middle of the night. I'd heard a doorbell. Really loud. Up close. Why would there be a doorbell in my bedroom?

Sputnik.

When I flicked the lamp on, there he was, sitting on the end of my bed, his portable doorbell in his hand.

– How did you get in here?

'Easy. I disabled the extremely primitive alarm system.'

As soon as he said that . . .

WHAAAAAA WHAAAAA

. . . the alarm went off.

I had to clatter down the fire escape and stand in the car park in my pyjamas while the Night Care

Team counted us and made sure there was no actual fire. It was freezing cold. The fat full moon looked down on us like a camera. Sputnik had refused to leave my room.

– What if there really is a fire?

'If there was a fire, I'd be able to smell it.'

By the time I got back to my room, Sputnik had grabbed the bed. He was lying there blowing randomly into Grandad's harmonica.

– Shh. You'll wake everyone.

'I'm playing a lullaby. I'll probably put everyone to sleep.'

– Only if they're deaf.

'So where's this sea chest then?'

– It's back at the old flat. But it's useless without the key. Grandad's got the key. If we want to open it, we have to find Grandad.

'I've thought about this,' said Sputnik. 'If he's not in jail, he's probably in Australia.'

– Australia?

'I've looked into it, and apparently when you've been really bad in this country, they send you to Australia. Let's go!'

– Australia is the other side of the world.

'There's an airport in Glasgow. I'm absolutely one hundred per cent confident that they'll lend us a plane. After all, it's their planet we're trying to save.'

– And when we get to Australia?

'We ask around till we find someone who knows your grandad. Someone's bound to. If he's a criminal, there will be criminal records.'

– You haven't found my grandad at all. You're just taking a wild guess.

'I have it on very good authority that if you do something too bad for jail they send you to Australia . . .'

– That was hundreds of years ago. They don't do that any more.

'So where's this map then?'

– What do you want the map for?

'To help me find your grandad.'

– It's not a map of where he is. It's a map of where he's been. And by the way, he's never been to Australia.

'The only way I know to find out where someone is, is to start where they used to be and move forward.'

I handed him the map.

Sputnik held it the right way up, with Murmansk

at the top. Then he held it upside down, with the Amazon at the top. Then he held it flat and looked straight across as if he thought there might be tiny Himalayas hidden in its folds. (There weren't.) He pressed it against the window.

'Turn out the light. I'm going to show you something.'

It was the middle of the night. The Temporary is up on top of a hill. When Sputnik held the map against the window, the light of the moon shone through like a pale headlamp.

'I don't think this,' said Sputnik, 'is a map of the world.' He moved it over the glass, as if he was hoping the moonlight would find something. 'I think this,' he said, 'is a map of your town. Look.'

He tugged the corners of the map. The map got bigger. Its paper got thinner. Soon the pattern of street lights shone through it. He tugged it a little bigger and thinner. Now I could see the separate points of the street lights. He shuffled the map around. The pattern of the street lights fitted perfectly over the lines of the streets on the map.

'This is not a map of the world,' said Sputnik. 'This is a map of Dumfries. Look . . . See where it says the Amazon? That's the River Nith running through the town. Where it says the Taj Mahal . . .'

– That's the Robbie Burns Memorial.

'The Leaning Tower of Pisa . . .'

– Which isn't leaning.

'Because it's actually Dumfries's famous Camera Obscura. And Murmansk with the drawing of the polar bear on the ice floes . . .'

– Is the ice rink. But . . . does that mean . . . ? It does mean . . . I haven't travelled to all those places. I haven't seen the world. I've never been anywhere but Dumfries.

'Dumfries is good. They don't call her Queen of the South for nothing.'

– But everything was lies. Why? Why would he do that?

'I don't know. We need to read between the lines.' He folded the map in half, then in half again. 'How many times do you think you could do this?'

I took it from him and folded it again and then one more time, but the paper was too small to fold any more, and the folds were too thick to bend. It took me all my strength to find out that I couldn't do it more than six times.

Sputnik took it back. He folded it a seventh time. Pressed it neatly into layers, and then folded

it again. It was tiny now. Not much bigger than a stamp, but thick as a sandwich.

'One more time?'

He folded it again. And then again. And again. Twelve times. Fifteen times. Eighteen times. Twenty-one. It got narrower and narrower but taller and taller. Until the map was a line strung out into the sky . . .

– Are you sure you'll be able to unfold this again?

'Just a few more folds.'

The map-string was so thin now I had to keep staring at it to stop it disappearing. If

I scrunched up my eyes I could just catch sight of it when it moved, like a spider's web when there's mist and sunlight. It snaked through the glass of the window and somehow I could see that it was squeezing itself between the molecules of glass.

'Are you counting?'

– If you fold it again, it'll be twenty-seven.

He folded it again.

There was a whoosh.

The glowing string rocketed up and up. I tried to see where it was going but it seemed to be going to forever. It flew away but it also stayed where it was, changing but the same, like a tiny, bright upwards waterfall of fireflies.

– What is it?

'People say that no matter how big a piece of paper is, you can't fold it more than seven times. But if you make the effort and keep folding, then when you get to twenty-seven times, you go atomic. This is still your grandad's map, but now you're looking at it one atom at a time. It stretches to the very edge of the solar system.'

I thought of Grandad's map stretching out to the edge of the solar system like the finest fishing line. I thought, if I could just tweak it, I might feel him tugging at the other end, and be able to reel him in. But my finger couldn't find it, even though I could still see it.

'If I kept on going to 103 folds,' said Sputnik, 'the other end of this map would be outside the known universe.'

– That is a long way.

'I do this whenever I get homesick,' said Sputnik. 'Get down to the atoms. Wherever you go in the universe, atoms are atoms. A hydrogen atom is a hydrogen atom and an oxygen atom is an oxygen atom. Whether it's here or a thousand galaxies away.'

– You get homesick? But you said you didn't have a home.

'You don't have to have a home to get homesick. You just have to want one. The whole history of your wee planet is nothing but people looking for a home. Look at those Vikings, charging off across the sea, waving their battleaxes, just looking for somewhere to call their own . . .'

– That's true.

'The Roman soldiers on that wall, building their baths and eating their olives in the mist and the rain, hundreds of miles from where they grew up, trying to make it feel like home. People crossing the sea in little boats looking for somewhere safe to land, somewhere to call their own. Remember Laika up in that rocket? She had the whole of space. What did she look at? Earth. The place where she grew up. Home.'

– What if you haven't got a place to look back at?

'Home's not a building. Home is other people, isn't it?'

– What if you haven't got other people?

'You have. Your grandad. Look . . .'

– I don't know where he is.

Sputnik tugged on the string of atoms, hauling it in, and gathering it up, unfolding what he'd folded until I could read the map again. He moved it around over the moonlight until it found a little patch of Grandad's writing just at the top of George Street.

'What does that say?'

It said 'Shangri-La'.

'Do you think there really is a mythical magical Himalayan mountain at the top of George Street that no one else has noticed?'

– No.

'Then you should probably go and see what really is there.'

22.
Shangri-La

I brushed my hair.

I put my uniform on.

Ate my breakfast.

Brushed my teeth.

Fixed myself a packed lunch. Said goodbye.

I did all the things you're supposed to do on a school morning. I walked to the corner, then nipped in behind the bus shelter and waited for Sputnik. He'd sneaked out down the fire escape.

'Got the map?' he asked.

I waved the map at him.

'Let's go. To Shangri-La!'

It was just a big house at the top end of George Street. The one next door had been turned into a hotel. Another one was flats. The Shangri-La was an old building with new windows and new gates. It had a front garden with a big swing seat and a bird table and a sign with a poem about gardens being like heaven. There was a kind of bike shelter off to one side. There were no steps up to the front door. Just a ramp.

– How can we get in without anyone seeing us?

'Why don't you want anyone to see us? Just ring the doorbell and ask.'

– Ask what?

'Ask them if they want you to take your old grandad away. They'll probably be only too glad to get rid of him, with him being a criminal and everything.'

I rang the bell. A nurse in a grey uniform with his hair pulled back into a tight ponytail came to the door.

He looked down at me. 'We don't do work experience, if that's what you're here about,' he said.

'I've come to see my grandad.'

'Visiting time doesn't start until four. What's your grandad's name?

'Mellows. Mr Mellows.'

'There's no one here by that name.'

'Are you sure? I really thought . . .'

But the man wasn't listening to me. Sputnik had

put his head on one side and was smiling with all his teeth.

'Well, aren't you just the best?' said the man, crouching down and chucking Sputnik under the chin.

'Yes, I am,' said Sputnik. 'The best. The very best at nearly everything.' He shook the man's hand.

'He understands every word. Every little word. You understand, don't you? Don't you?'

Even if Sputnik had been an actual dog, the way he went on would have been a bit much.

'What's your name? What's your name? What's your little name?'

'You don't need to know my name,' said Sputnik. 'You need to listen to this . . .'

And he whistled a loud clear piercing whistle. He whistled 'Flower of Scotland'. The nurse stood up and took a step back. His eyes almost exploded.

'Elsa!' he called. 'Elsa, you have to see this! The residents have to see it. The world has to see it. Come in. Come in. My name's Gregory by the way. I'm so, so pleased to meet you.' Gregory, it seemed, was a man who had waited all his life to meet a whistling dog.

*

264

Elsa turned out to be the boss. She agreed completely with Gregory that the old people had to hear Sputnik whistle. Right now. She made it sound like a whistling dog might possibly be the cure for being old.

So that's how we got in.

Straight into the lounge.

A big room with big windows open on to a garden. A big telly on, showing *MasterChef* on maximum volume, with subtitles for the hard of hearing. Chairs all around the walls. An old person in every chair. Some of them asleep. Some of them watching the telly. And one of them leaning forward in his seat shouting, 'That's no how you chop an onion!' at the man on the telly. It was my grandad.

He was not in jail at all. He was just sitting in an armchair, in the breeze from the French windows.

Shangri-La – it turns out – is an old people's home. Just an old people's home.

23.
Stairlift

It was ages since I'd really wanted to tell anyone
anything. But I was bursting to tell Grandad . . .
everything.

All about the Blythes.

About how I'd thought he was in jail.

Even about Sputnik.

Just the feeling of wanting to talk was exciting.

'Grandad!' I said. 'They said you weren't
here.'

'This is your grandad?' said Gregory. 'But his
name's not Mellows. It's Mala . . . Mela . . . Hang
on, I never get this right . . .'

Grandad turned away from the telly and looked
me straight in the eye. 'Meletxea,' he said. 'It's
Basque. It means "home in the hills".'

Grandad must be really confused today. Even
on the bad days when he couldn't remember my

name, he'd know his own. 'No,' I said, 'your name is Mellows.'

'Mellows was my wife's name. I used it because I couldn't be bothered spelling out Meletxea to people all the time. Meletxea. It means "home in the hills".'

My mind couldn't keep up with this news. 'So, that means that my name is Mela . . . Mala . . . unpronounceable too? That my name isn't what I thought it was? I'm not even Prez Mellows?' But Grandad wasn't listening.

'Don't slash at the onions like that!'

Gregory wasn't listening either. He was too busy gathering the other residents. 'No one should miss this.'

'Don't start without us,' said Elsa.

'There's a dog! A dog in the room!' shouted a man in a bright yellow cardigan.

'The dog is the entertainment,' said Gregory.

'Just you wait and see,' said Elsa.

'AN ONION IS NOT MADE OF WOOD! DON'T SAW IT! CHOP IT!' yelled Grandad.

'Grandad,' I said, 'it's me!'

'Oh!' He stared at me. 'Ah. You came. That's great. Everyone, listen! He's here! He's finally here.'

All the other residents looked at me. I waved at

them. The man in the yellow cardigan waved back. A couple of the others said I was very welcome. The woman in the next chair whispered very loud, 'Who is it?'

'This,' said Grandad, pointing at me, 'is the electrician I was telling you about.'

Everyone seemed to be pleased to hear this.

'He fixes light bulbs, light switches, anything you want to name. He's a chuffing genius. Going to fix the telly, aren't you, bud?'

Bud?

So.

He didn't know who I was.

My grandad had forgotten me.

'Well, say something.'

What could I say?

'What's wrong with the telly?' asked Sputnik. If you ever wanted to get Sputnik's attention, all you had to do was mention that some electrical item wasn't working.

'What is wrong with the telly, Grandad?' I was hoping that if I kept calling him Grandad he might remember who I was.

'I've been trying to attract this chap's attention all morning.' He pointed to the chef on the screen. 'He can't seem to hear me. I think one of the speakers mustn't be working.'

'Grandad, tellies aren't two-way. You can hear him, but he can't hear you.'

'Exactly. That's exactly the problem. You've put your finger on it. See how he put his finger on the problem right away? I told you he was good. Now go on and fix it.'

'Not really, Grandad. Tellies can't hear.'

'Have you got the manual?' said Sputnik.

'That's not how tellies work.'

'You say that about everything,' said Sputnik. 'Where's the manual?' There actually was a manual for once, in a clear plastic cover on top of the telly. Sputnik flicked through it. 'Seems straightforward enough,' he said, wrenching the back off the television. He dug around in his backpack for a screwdriver.

'I think you should disconnect it before you do anything to it.'

'You always make such a fuss,' said Sputnik. Then he said, 'OW!' Electric sparks showered around him. His sporran blazed. 'Brilliant,' he said, patting the fire out with his bare hands. 'That's that all sorted. Do I smell something edible or is that my smouldering sporran? Anyway, all you need to do now is press the red button. He should be able to hear you.'

The chef was back on the telly. He'd stopped chopping onions now and was cutting courgettes into twisty strips with some kind of gadget.

'WHA—?! I'VE SAILED THE SEVEN SEAS WITH CRIMINALS AND KINGS BUT THAT'S THE MOST AMAZING THING I'VE EVER SEEN!'

'Grandad, it really doesn't . . .'

But the telly chef had stopped spiralizing. He was looking up in the air, and behind him, as if he could hear a voice.

'OVER HERE!' yelled Grandad.

The chef looked straight into camera. He seemed to be looking into the room. 'Hello?' he said.

'WHERE CAN I GET ONE OF THEM SPIRAL THINGS? I WANT ONE.'

'Mel,' said the chef, 'is this supposed to be happening?' A man in a set of headphones stepped into view and looked into the camera. Grandad waved at him. Mel looked very puzzled but he was too polite not to wave back.

By now all the residents were crowding round

the telly, staring into the screen. 'Well, go on,' said Grandad. 'Give them a wave.'

All the residents gave the telly a big old wave. Mel and the chef waved back.

'Is this some kind of prank?' asked the chef.

'WHERE CAN WE GET ONE OF THOSE TWISTY THINGS?'

'The spiralizer is available from all good stores,' said the chef. 'Is this some kind of joke?'

'I think it's to do with interactivity,' said Mel. 'Are you people watching us on your TV?'

All the residents said yes, they were. Some of them clapped their hands. They were loving this.

'Could we possibly ask you to be quiet? Or perhaps to change channel? We do have a show to get through.'

'Could we switch to a channel with that George Clooney on?' said the lady in the chair next to Grandad's. 'I like him.'

'Can't change channel. We've lost the remote. Don't mind us!' called Grandad. He patted me on the head. 'I told you he was a great electrician,' he said. Then he asked, 'What's your name, son?'

I looked away so he wouldn't see if I got upset. It was a good job I did look away, because I was just in time to spot Sputnik slipping out into the hall. He had found the stairlift.

He was standing in the middle of the hallway, hands on his hips, watching Gregory and Elsa help a shaky old lady on to a kind of big metal chair attached to a rail at the top of the stairs. Once she was safely strapped in, the chair chugged into position, then slowly, slowly glided downstairs, its lullaby motor humming.

'That,' said Sputnik, 'is disappointingly slow.'

– It's supposed to be slow. It's for old people.

'Old people don't want to go slow. They've got hardly any time left. They've got to make the most of it. I'm going to look into this. I must say, I'm very glad we came here. The place is full of electrical challenges.'

The old lady climbed out of the chair and patted him on the head. 'Is this him?' she said. 'How exciting. I've heard *of* a dog whistle, but I've never heard a dog whistle.'

Sputnik didn't reply. He was already tinkering with the motor. The chair slid back up the stairs. An old man in a bow tie was waiting to get on board. He lay his walking stick across his knees and told Gregory he was ready.

'That should work,' said Sputnik.

– What have you done?

Gregory threw the switch. The stairlift whined. For a second the old man looked worried, then he looked blurred. The chair shot down the stairs like a bullet. It screeched to a halt at the bottom. The old man's bow tie was undone. His eyes blazed like a pair of moons.

'A definite improvement,' said Sputnik.

'Mr Leithen!' Elsa gasped. 'Are you OK?'

Mr Leithen looked up the stairs.

Mr Leithen looked at his feet.

Mr Leithen checked his bow tie.

He was trying to figure out where he was. And how he'd got there so fast.

Then he said, 'Again. Do it again.'

Elsa was fussing with his safety belt. 'Let me help you out. I'm so sorry. I've no idea how that happened.'

'Again,' said Mr Leithen again. 'I want to do it again.'

'We'll have you out in no time.'

'I don't want to get out!' Mr Leithen poked her away with his walking stick. 'I want to do it again.'

'No problem,' said Sputnik. He flicked the

switch. Like a rocket the chair zoomed up the stairs. 'This. Is. The. Finest. Thing. Ever!' whooped Mr Leithen. 'Again. Again!'

By now there was a queue of old people waiting to come down. When Mr Leithen said he wanted another go, they were all furious. 'No, no!' they yelled. 'It's my turn. Me next!'

Elsa was nearly in tears. 'I don't understand what's going on,' she said to me. 'Please accept my apologies. Please give us a moment to sort out these technical difficulties. I hope your dog is not too upset.'

There were times when it was a relief that people thought Sputnik was just an innocent pet doggy and not what he actually was.

Back in the day room the rest of the residents were still crowded around the telly. But Grandad was back in his chair, dreaming about the courgette spiralizer. 'I've had knives and I've had graters. I had a potato peeler that was so good I wouldn't let it out of my sight. But in all my puff I have never seen anything like that.'

I went to him. I thought that now it was just the

two of us, and everyone else was busy, something might click. He smiled at me.

'Do you think they do electric spiralizers?' he said. 'Could you get me one?'

I didn't know what to say.

But I thought I knew what to do.

I took the map out of my pocket, unfolded it and put it on his lap. He looked at it. He frowned. 'Where,' he growled, 'did you get this?'

He didn't give me a chance to answer. He leaned forward in his chair. He put his finger on the corner of the map. 'This is a private map. This map is private between me and someone else. Where did you get it? Have you been going through my sea chest?'

I shook my head.

'Gregory! There's a thief in the house! A burglar!'

Gregory didn't come. He had his hands full trying to stop pensioners speeding on the stairs.

'Grandad, you drew this map. You drew it for *me*. You said we went to all these places in the world. Except it's not a map of the world; it's a map of Dumfries. You must remember.'

'Gregory!'

Still Gregory didn't come.

But Sputnik came.

He said, 'OK. I found your grandad. Now you have to show me this last wonderful thing and I can go.'

– I haven't found my grandad. He's still lost.

'He's sitting right in front of you.'

– He doesn't know who I am.

Then I had a thought:

– You're good at fixing things. He's broken. Can you fix him?

'People aren't stairlifts. You can't just fix them. People don't come with a manual.'

– I said that to you once. About backpacks. You still made mine fly.

'And talking of making things fly . . .' He was staring out of the French windows. A lady in a pink cardigan was riding one of those mobility scooters across the lawn. 'Why didn't you bring me here before? This place has all the best stuff.' And he was gone.

'Greg-o-ryyyy!!!' called Grandad.

Gregory and Elsa came in, herding four very excited old people in front of them. The old people were talking non-stop about the new, improved express stairlift. Elsa was trying to keep things calm. 'We've had a bit of excitement this morning, but now we can all calm down and enjoy the whistling dog. Where is the whistling dog?'

She looked around for Sputnik. She didn't see him. What she did see was most of the residents of Shangri-La standing around the telly, yelling. The cookery show was over now and there was one of those programmes where people shout at each other about private stuff. The old people were all really angry about the people on the screen. The presenter was looking into the camera, 'Please,' he pleaded, 'whoever you are, please stop shouting. We can't hear our guests shouting.'

'What on earth is going on here?' said Elsa. 'We've got a special surprise for you all. Please, ladies and gentlemen, do go and sit down.'

'Excuse me! Are you in charge here?'

Elsa looked around but couldn't see who was talking.

'Yeah, she's in charge,' said Yellow Cardigan Man.

'Can you get everyone to calm down, please?' said the voice. 'This is supposed to be a thoughtful, respectful programme.'

'Who's talking? Where are you?'

'Over here. On the telly.'

Elsa stared at the telly. On the screen, the presenter pointed right at her and yelled, 'Are you Elsa and are you here to help?'

'What?' gasped Elsa. 'How did you know my name?'

'You're wearing a badge,' said the man on the telly. 'It says, "I'm Elsa and I'm here to help."'

Elsa glanced down at her own name badge. 'But you're on telly,' she said. 'How can you see me?'

'I've stopped trying to keep up with the marvels of technology,' said the presenter. 'All I know is you're making too much noise.'

Elsa turned the television off. Then she stood for a while with her eyes closed, concentrating on her breathing. Gregory came in and gave her a peppermint, which he said was good for the nerves. She shook her arms and shook her head and said, 'Calm, calm, be mindful,' to herself as she walked to the window. 'What is this life if, full of care, we have no time to stand and stare.' She stared out of the window, smiling at the flowers. She did not smile at what happened next.

A shower of glass cascaded through the air and pattered on to the patio.

There was a loud scream.

Then there was the stairlift. Except it wasn't on the stairs any more. It was barrelling through the air like a massive drunken bird. Snapping apple-tree branches as it powered onwards and upwards.

The screams were coming from Mr Leithen. They weren't really screams. They were cheers. 'Look at me!' he whooped. 'I'm flying!'

He'd sneaked back to the stairlift on his own to have an extra go. He'd pressed the button so hard it had blasted up the rails, straight through the skylight and into the sky.

'We have lift-off,' Sputnik said with a smile.

'He's going to crash!' wailed Elsa.

'Why don't you people ever read the instructions?' sniffed Sputnik. 'Look.'

The flying stairlift seemed to stall in the air, wobble, then lurch backwards. A gorgeous blue-and-white parachute blossomed above it. The wind caught it and wafted it sideways. Mr Leithen waved as his stairlift dilly-dallied over the orchard and danced down towards the gardens.

'Gregory,' snarled Grandad, 'this electrician fella has stolen my personal property.' He had hold of me by the elbow.

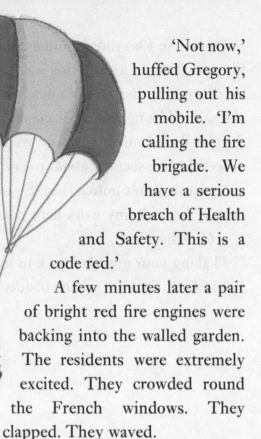

'Not now,' huffed Gregory, pulling out his mobile. 'I'm calling the fire brigade. We have a serious breach of Health and Safety. This is a code red.'

A few minutes later a pair of bright red fire engines were backing into the walled garden. The residents were extremely excited. They crowded round the French windows. They clapped. They waved.

'This is better than George Clooney,' said the lady next to Grandad.

Sputnik looked up at Elsa and said, 'When I first heard about a magical mystical land where no one got old and everyone was happy, I didn't believe a word of it. But now that I've been here I can see that it's partly right anyway. Everyone here *is* happy. Well done.'

Of course Elsa didn't understand a word of this. She just thought a small dog was barking at her. She sat down with her head in her hands, looked at me and said, 'The upset here is upsetting your poor wee doggy. We're normally very well organized. And peaceful.' She seemed about to cry.

Sputnik didn't notice this. 'So long as everyone's happy,' he said, 'my work here is done. Let's go.'

– Go where?'

'Taking your grandad back to his sea chest,' said Sputnik, 'to find out what's inside.'

24.
Teeth

Even though he didn't know who I was, he seemed to know where we were going. Grandad dragged one of the mobility scooters out of its shelter and climbed on. 'I'm not supposed to use this unsupervised. But if a fully qualified electrician isn't supervision, I don't know what is. Hop on the back,' he said. 'Next stop: Traquair Gardens.'

Sputnik sat between me and Grandad as we chugged over the bridge and down the river walk. That's the way we used to come home when he collected me from school, the way we went when he was doing his high-tide walks, the way we went if we were going to church. It felt good to be out in the fresh air with Grandad, even if he didn't know who I was.

When we got to Traquair Gardens, Mrs Mackie was smoking out of her window again, as if she'd never moved, as if smoking cigarettes was what she did for a living.

'Are you back for your stuff, Sandy Mellows? You've enough of it.'

Bags and boxes of Grandad's clutter was now piled up in the area in front of the house. The people who were moving in had finally cleared it all out, ready for collection.

A tottering pile of newspapers was leaning like the Tower of Pisa, against the steps. 'I'll be wanting them,' said Grandad.

'We've come for your sea chest, Grandad,' I reminded him.

'Aye, in due course. In the meantime there's all this to think about.' He pointed to a big box full of broken light bulbs. 'And where's my box of teeth?'

'Have you got the key to the sea chest with you, Grandad?'

'Aye, never without it.'

There was no sign of the sea chest outside. Maybe the new people had seen my Post-it note and were keeping it safe indoors. I was going to knock and ask, but Sputnik was too excited to wait. He tried the door. It opened. The smell of fresh paint and disinfectant breezed out. The hallway had been painted a fresh, buttery yellow. Everywhere was so clean and bright. It made me think that the new people must be really nice, even though they had stolen our house.

Sputnik dashed inside.

The fact that the door wasn't locked should have warned me what was going to happen. But I was too busy thinking about Sputnik and the sea chest. I felt bad that he was so excited about it. I'd made him think it held the Tenth Wonder of the World, when for all I knew it was full of old socks and razors. Or more false teeth.

'It's here!' yelled Sputnik. 'Come on, Grandad. Time to open up!'

But Grandad was quietly sorting through the pile of newspapers. '7 June 2012 is missing,' he called. The way he said it, it sounded as if an entire day had dropped out of history, rather than just one copy of the *Scotsman*. He was looking around for some sign of the lost day.

'I really want to see what's in this sea chest. Is it all right if I chivvy him in here at gunpoint?'

– No!

Just then Grandad came speeding past us, tugging a chain out from under his shirt. There was a little key on the chain. 'Where's that chest?' he muttered.

'Maybe the missing *Scotsman* is in there.'

He pushed open the door of what used to be his bedroom. It was completely empty apart from a couple of boxes. The floor was bare wooden boards. The walls were painted pale blue. I thought he would be upset, but he just said, 'Aye, this'll do nicely. Start bringing all my stuff in, would you?'

Then he went over to the two boxes. One of them was his sea chest. The other was the one marked 'Teeth'. He opened the teeth box first. I was expecting it to be full of old sets of false teeth, but the first thing he took out was the jaw of a shark, bristling with wicked sharp fangs.

'Got that in the South Seas,' he said. 'Swapped it for cigarettes.'

Then he took out a tooth the size of a fist covered in intricate carvings.

'That's from a walrus,' he said. 'Carved it myself. You had to find something to do with your hands on those Arctic trips.' He found a red pouch with a single yellow dog's tooth inside.

'You know what that is? When I was in Moscow that time, I found a wee stray. She was in agony from a bad tooth. I whipped it out with my little knife and she followed me everywhere from then on.

I fed her and washed her. Looked after her. She was a bonnie wee thing. I taught her to play fetch. I had a red rubber ball. No matter how far I threw it, she'd always bring it back. I even taught her to salute like a proper sailor. I wanted to bring her home with me, but they wouldn't let me. Took her off me before I got back on board. Made me fill in all kinds of forms. I was down in the mouth about that, but a year later I got a letter from a Russian navy officer who said he'd taken her out of the dog pound and – you'll not believe this – he'd trained her up and sent her into space. I think it was probably the salute that swung it for her. If you're going to send a dog up in a rocket, you want it to be one that can salute. Laika. That was her name, and this is her tooth.'

Sputnik looked amazed. 'You . . . you knew Laika?' he stammered. Then his amazement seemed to turn to fright. Grandad didn't have time to answer, and I didn't have time to ask what was wrong.

A woman came in through the door carrying a pot of paint. Seeing us there, she dropped the paint and screamed.

'Be calm, woman,' said Sputnik. 'We're having an exchange of information that might be crucial to the survival of your planet.'

Of course that's not what she heard. What she heard was *woof woof woof woof!*

Grandad stared at her and seemed to half remember something. 'Have I done it again?' he said. 'Is this not my house? I'm sorry, hen. Here, let me show you how to chop vegetables really fast. Pay particular careful attention.' His hand went up to his top pocket.

'Grandad, NO!!!'

It was too late. He'd taken out his wee vegetable knife. She'd seen it. Screamed louder than ever. A man came running in. Called the police. A few seconds later we were all in the back of a police car.

One of the policemen asked Grandad if he was from the Shangri-La.

'Shangri-La,' said Grandad, 'doesn't exist. It's a mythical country invented for the film *Lost Horizon*. I think it was a book before that.'

'It's also the name of a home here in Dumfries, a special place for old people who are getting bit mixed up,' explained the policeman.

'Well, that counts me out,' said Grandad. 'Nothing mixed up about me. Never felt less mixed up in all my puff. Ask me anything.'

They asked him where he lived.

'I'm between addresses at the moment,' said Grandad. 'As you can see, I've got my luggage with me.' He had his sea chest on his knee. 'I don't think that's any reason to shove me in a home for bewildered pensioners, do you?'

The two policemen were beginning to look as if it might be possible for Grandad to convince them. The first one said, 'Just say, for instance, we didn't drop you at the Shangri-La . . . Where would we drop you?'

'Wherever's convenient for you. I'm not a baby. I can find my own way.'

The second cop said, 'What about the dog?'

'What dog?'

'The dog on the back seat, sitting between you.'

'There's no dog back here, son. I think you must be dreaming.'

'Yes. He's sitting up between the two of you.'

'You need your eyes testing, bud,' said Grandad. 'That's not a dog. That's my very good friend Sputnik Mellows. What dog would wear a kilt? Or a flying helmet? Or a pair of goggles, I ask you.'

That Grandad could see Sputnik . . . really see him . . . kilt, goggles, flying helmet, the lot . . . that was the best thing ever.

All through the amazing things I'd done with Sputnik – flying, floating, foiling robberies – there was a background buzz of loneliness that I hadn't even noticed until it stopped. The loneliness of not being able to tell anyone about it.

Now I had someone to talk to, that background buzz was gone, like when your ears pop after swimming.

But . . .

That Grandad could see Sputnik was also, obviously, the worst thing ever. As soon as he said it, the two policemen looked at each other, nodded, and a few minutes later Grandad and his sea chest were back in Shangri-La.

They took me back to the Temporary.

They took Sputnik to the dog pound.

So by the time it got dark that night all three of us were behind locked doors.

25.
Grandad's Harmonica

When Murder Bell heard that I'd stolen a vehicle he was impressed.

When he heard that the vehicle was a mobility scooter he laughed so loud I could hear him three rooms away.

When you do something bad at the Temporary – for instance coming home in a police car – they make you write a list of promises. They call it 'The Contract'.

You're supposed to come up with your own promises, but I got a lot of help this time from Mrs Rowland.

1. I promise that if I'm worried about my grandad or anyone else, I will ASK about them. I will not attempt to kidnap Grandad again, using a vehicle that does not belong to me and an unpredictable dog.

If I don't want to talk, that's OK. I can ASK by text, Facebook, WhatsApp or Post-it note. But I will ASK.

2. I promise not to take other people's mobility scooters - or any other vehicles - without permission or supervision.

3. If I want to go into someone else's house for whatever reason, I promise that I will ASK. I will not do breaking and entering.

4. If I do any breaking and entering - which I won't - I promise not to get bewildered old men or unpredictable dogs involved in my crime.

5. I agree that my grandad is someone who needs constant professional adult supervision due to his habit of pulling a knife on people. I do not count as a professional adult supervisor.

6. If a dog - or any other stray animal - turns up at the Children's Temporary

Accommodation, I promise to inform the staff and not try to hide the animal under my bed.

7. Not talking to people is fine. But if I upset people or mess them about it's my job to put things right. It's up to me to find a way to do that, even without talking (see Promise 1).

In order to help me keep Promise 7, Mrs Rowland came and got me when Ray and Jessie turned up next afternoon after tea. She said, 'This is your chance to put things right with this very nice family who have been so good to you.'

They were waiting in the hallway.

'Is this where you live normally?' said Ray. 'Nice being in the middle of town. Have you got your own room?'

Before I could answer, Jessie said, 'Sputnik's gone missing. We woke up this morning and there was no sign of him. We came here on the bus. Like you and me did that day.'

'Jessie thinks Sputnik got the bus too. I tried to tell her—'

'Sputnik would follow you to the end of the world,' said Jessie. 'Everyone knows that. Is he here?'

The point of Promise 7 is that I have to explain things. I was honestly about to do that when Mrs Rowland said, 'Yes, he did follow Prez all the way here. Though Prez never told us, did you, Prez?'

I was going to explain that too, but there was no stopping Mrs Rowland. 'And having followed him here, he then followed Prez to the nursing home where his grandad was staying, where Prez then took his grandad walkies.'

'That was nice of him,' said Ray.

'It may sound nice,' said Mrs Rowland, 'until you hear where he took him walkies to. Do you want to tell them, Prez?'

Yes, I did want to tell them. But not as much as Mrs Rowland wanted to tell them. 'He took them to the flat where he used to live and the three of them strolled right in there and started helping themselves to things.'

'Stealing?!' Jessie gasped.

'NO!' I shouted. I really didn't want Ray to think I was a thief.

'Well, not stealing exactly.' Mrs Rowland was flustered. She explained that we hadn't taken anything, but that Grandad had threatened the new people with a knife.

'He threatened them? Really? Isn't he a bit old and frail?' said Ray. 'He can't have been that much of a threat.'

'His grandad gets mixed up,' said Jessie. 'Doesn't he, Prez?'

They were sticking up for me. In the middle of all the bad stuff that felt good. So I said, 'He wanted to show her the quickest way to chop carrots.'

'At least we've found Sputnik though, eh?' Jessie smiled. 'Where is he? Is he in the garden?'

'As you know, we don't allow pets.'

'So . . .'

'So we called the police and they took him away.'

'What?! Why didn't you call *us*?' wailed Jessie.

'Because,' said Mrs Rowland, 'I had enough to do persuading the police not to press charges against Prez. For breaking and entering. And threatening behaviour. I could go on . . .'

I hadn't thought of that. She'd probably had to work hard to keep me out of trouble. I remembered my manners and said, 'Thank you.'

'Right. We'd better go and try to get him back,' said Ray. 'See you, Prez.'

They left. Just like that. Seeing them had been like going back to Stramoddie for two minutes.

When they went, the Temporary seemed bigger and emptier than ever.

So it was good when the door opened and Ray stuck his head round it, saying, 'It's OK if Prez comes with us, isn't it?'

'Well, I suppose so,' said Mrs Rowland. 'But do bring him back when you're finished with him. I'd miss him if he wasn't here.'

We walked round to the police station together. They didn't speak to each other. We didn't speak. Jessie and Ray seemed to know what each other was thinking, what they were going to say.

They didn't know what I was thinking though. I was thinking about the crunchy drifts of red and gold leaves along the pavement. Leaves that had fallen from the trees. Leaves that said, Very soon this planet will shrink.

The police station smelt mostly of disinfectant and coffee but if I concentrated I could just catch a faint whiff of dog.

There was a really crabbit police officer at the desk. 'What's the name of the missing animal?' she said.

'Sputnik,' said Jessie.

'That's not the name on the collar of the dog we're holding,' said the officer. She was looking through a giant notebook she'd pulled out from under the desk.

'Oh. The collar,' said Ray. 'It's not his collar. It was the collar of our old dog. This dog is a stray.'

'He just turned up,' said Jessie. 'We thought he might belong to someone so we Facebooked about him.'

'Under Scottish law a dog is required to wear a collar with the name and address of the owner and the dog clearly displayed on it.'

'But he *is* wearing a collar. You just told us that.'

'But you've just told me it's not *his* collar. You're also required to keep him under control, which you clearly did not do or he wouldn't be here. If you want him back, you have to sign an agreement.'

'No problem,' said Ray.

'How old are you?'

'Sixteen. Nearly seventeen.'

'Then you have got a problem. You have to be eighteen to sign.'

'That's OK,' said Ray. 'We're happy to wait here till I'm eighteen. Mind if we sit down?'

The police officer gave him a look.

'Could we not just go and see if he's all right?' said Jessie. 'The one you have might not even be the right dog.'

It was already getting dark out in the car park behind the police station. There were a couple of police cars, a Portakabin, and, standing in a big puddle in the darkest corner, a metal cage. Its bars were covered in wire mesh.

At first I thought Sputnik wasn't in there. Then I noticed a pile of wet clothes in the corner. It was him, curled up in a heap, clutching his backpack. His eyes were cold. They'd tied a bit of rope to his collar and tied the other end to the bars of the cage, using a clove hitch knot.

In all our times together, the thing that Sputnik was the most was noisy. He was a shouting, singing, crashing, exploding whirlwind of racket. I'd never seen him quiet before.

'That's him, but he looks so sad!' said Jessie. 'Can't we take him?'

'Not without signing the paperwork. Which you're not old enough to do.'

'But what's going to happen to him?'

298

'As you admitted yourselves, he is a stray and as such we'll be asking the Animal Rescue to take him. If they say no, I shall take steps to have him destroyed.'

'Destroyed?!' howled Jessie. 'No. Please.'

'It's OK,' said Ray. 'I'll call our mum. I'm sure she'll sign.'

'She'll be in a fury,' said Jessie.

'She'll be in a fury on the phone, but she'll calm down on the drive over.'

There wasn't much signal out in the car park. They went inside to use the police phone and I stayed behind with Sputnik.

– I'm really sorry you got arrested.

He didn't answer.

– I know this is probably not the best moment but . . . you know . . . the list? To save the planet?

'Forget it.'

– I can't just forget it. I live on it. I keep all my stuff here. I have to try to save it. We've got nine things. We just need—

'It's not like it was going to last much longer anyway.'

– What?!

'Even if we had managed to save it for now, I'd still only give it another thirty million years tops.'

That's loads of time. That's the whole of history times thirty.

'It sounds a lot, but it's less time than it takes starlight to cross a galaxy. It's the twinkling of an eye. Literally. Anyway, it's all over now. So I'm getting out of here before the Big Shrink. Have you got your knife on you?'

– But you can't just *leave*. You promised to look after me.

'Ah. Sorry. Should've said. That was a misunderstanding. I was never supposed to be looking after you at all. Even Sputnik can make mistakes. Apparently. Please. Cut the rope.'

– What?! A misunderstanding?! What *kind* of misunderstanding?

'Don't worry. It wasn't your fault.'

– I know it's not my fault. Obviously it's not my fault! How could it be my fault?

'There was just a bit of a mix-up. I'm going to make up for it. I'm going to make you a special offer. When you've cut the rope.'

So I took out the knife that Grandad gave me and I cut through his rope. He rolled his head around, trying to relax his neck.

– A special offer to make up for my planet collapsing? What kind of special offer?

'Come with me.'

– What?

'You can come with me. Round the universe. Like a comet. Your whole world collapses but it won't matter what happens to your planet because you'll still have . . . . me.'

I thought about this for about ten seconds. I thought about shooting stars and nebulae and oceans made of gas. I didn't know how it would work, but I knew it would be mad and marvellous. Everything to do with Sputnik was mad and marvellous.

I said, out loud, 'No. Thanks. But no.'

'What?! You know your planet is going to shrink to nothing?'

– Someone's got to look after Grandad. When I saw him in that place, I thought, They don't know how he likes his tea. They don't know how to calm him down when he gets upset. They don't take him for walks.

'The whole world's going to collapse. You don't need to worry about his tea.'

– If the whole world's going to collapse, then

I really want him to have a nice cup of tea.

'He doesn't even know who you are.'

– But I know who *he* is.

Sputnik didn't say anything else except goodbye. Oh. And he gave me back Grandad's harmonica. 'Maybe he'll want to play you a tune.'

Back in the police station I could hear Jessie and Ray arguing with their mum on the phone. She must have said something about how there was no point taking Sputnik back because Sputnik didn't want to live on the farm, he wanted to live with me, because Jessie was saying, 'Then why doesn't Prez live with us too? That will solve everything.'

Ray said, 'Jessie, you can't ask a person to live with you just because you want to share his dog.'

'There's other things I like about him apart from his dog. You like him too, Mum. He empties the dishwasher! He collects the eggs. He makes a really good tomato sauce. Please . . .'

There was a long pause. I wasn't sure I wanted to hear the reply. So I put my hand up and said, 'Don't worry about Sputnik,' out loud. They all looked at me – Jessie, Ray and the crabbit police officer. 'Sputnik,' I said, 'has got plans of his own.'

'What kind of plans?' asked Ray.

But before I could reply, a noise drowned me out. Not a noise I expected to hear in a police station. I could see that none of the others knew what it was. But I knew right away. I'd heard it before, at a birthday party weeks ago. It was the sound of a red lightsaber blazing through metal.

It stopped. A loud clang. Metal bouncing on to a stone floor.

The bars of the cage had been sliced like a banana. They rolled and rang across the ground. The hot tang of burnt metal hung in the air.

'What happened?'

'Where's Sputnik?'

Everyone looked at me. As if I might know. Which of course I did.

Jessie started to cry. 'You said you were looking after him! Now he's gone!'

The police officer was looking all around the yard but she wasn't looking for Sputnik. 'There was a police car here a minute ago,' she said. 'An emergency response vehicle. It was parked right there.'

She pointed to the empty space.

The moment she pointed, a siren started and a bright-yellow-and-blue police van went screaming past the gate.

26.
Postcards

'You know,' said Ray as they walked me back to the Temporary, 'Sputnik strayed into Stramoddie – maybe he's just decided to stray somewhere else. Some people are like that. They don't want to settle. They like to wander. We're just blessed that he stayed with us for a while. Maybe I'll do that when I leave school – just wander around the world, try and see it all. And the people I meet, well, they'll be blessed to have met me.'

It was late by the time they left me at the Temporary. The mum was waiting for them outside in the car. I could tell Jessie and Ray were in trouble for going off to Dumfries without telling anyone, but she was nice to me. She said I was welcome any time. Then she drove off.

I went to my room, waited until the house went quiet, then sneaked out on to the fire escape to see if I could spot anything unusual in the vicinity of Sirius. Even the stars looked different now he'd gone. When you looked up at night in Stramoddie the sky was velvet smothered in luminous caster sugar. When you looked up in the town, it was just a few hundred specks of paint on a blackboard.

When Sputnik went he took half the galaxy with him.

I wanted to talk and talk and talk about him. I was scared that if I didn't, I might forget all about him. There was only one person I could talk to though. The only other person who had ever seen him.

Grandad.

I'd promised Mrs Rowland that if I was worried about Grandad I would say so. I texted her that I wanted to see him. She texted me ☺, phoned the Shangri-La Nursing Home and even gave me a lift.

Elsa seemed pleased to see me. 'Last time you came,' she said with a smile, 'we were having a slight stairlift malfunction. But that's all sorted out now. Your grandad's waiting for you in the day room. I'll take you through.'

But he wasn't in the day room.

'Oh. Perhaps he's getting some air on the patio.'

No.

'The garden room maybe?'

Not there either.

'He must have gone back to his room. He sometimes gets muddled up about what time it is. I'll go up and check.'

I followed her up the stairs.

'You don't need to come. I'll bring him down,' she said. 'We've got tea and cakes in the lounge.'

One of the good things about not talking is you don't have to explain why you're not doing as you're told. I followed her up to Grandad's room.

The room was neat and bare. Not like the cluttery cave he'd made in his bedroom back at Traquair Gardens. It had a bed, a bedside table and a wardrobe.

It did not have a grandad.

'Don't worry. He can't be far away.'

Oh yes, he can, I thought. There were some postcards and a school photo of me on the bedside table. They were views of Rumblecairn Bay.

Elsa saw me looking at them. 'We got those for him. We've been explaining to him who you are and where you've been. Hopefully he'll know who you are when we find him. We work very hard to reconnect them with their happy memories. We use music. Poetry. It's amazing how the mind works. Even when it's not working properly. Come on. Hide and seek.'

But I'd noticed something else. One of the postcards was marking a page in a little book. I picked it up. *The Solway Firth Tide Timetable*. The page it was marking was today. One high tide was underlined.

Rumblecairn Bay – 15.33

And Grandad wasn't the only thing missing from the room.

The sea chest wasn't there either.

Grandad had run away to sea.

I thought to myself, what would Sputnik do?

Then I realized he would probably do something that involved high explosives and danger to life and limb.

I had to think of a plan of my own.

Elsa left me in the garden room, with a plate of shortcake, some teacups and a promise she'd be back with Grandad in half a mo. Mr Leithen was standing at the window, watching the blue tits on the bird feeder. Without turning round, he whispered, 'Your grandad's done a runner.'

I didn't answer. I thought I might have imagined it. He said, 'He sent his sea chest down on the stairlift during breakfast. Strapped it on the back of one of the mobility scooters and vamoosed. Made a break for it. He's escaped.'

I knew he was telling the truth.

I had two hours to high tide, but Rumblecairn was hours and hours away. I didn't want to think about what would happen to him if he got as far as the bay at high tide. I had no plan. I just had to get going.

'If you'd just give us a moment,' said Elsa, 'we'll check the toilets. They sometimes get locked in.'

I nodded, smiled and as soon as her back was turned dashed out of the front door and down the drive.

I'd only just turned on to George Street when an electric hooter parped behind me. A mobility scooter was trying to get past. The driver was Mr Leithen. 'Get on,' he said.

A mobility scooter? To catch a runaway grandad?

'He's on a mobility scooter himself. I'm a better

driver than he is. What are your options? Come on. Hop on the back. Let's do this!'

I think the most I've ever missed Sputnik was when I was sitting on the back of that mobility scooter as it chugged slowly, slowly over the bridge and inched up the hill towards the bypass. I just know he would have adjusted its engine so that it could fly or go supersonic or destroy every car in its path. That day, the most exciting it got was when a milk float pulled up alongside us at the lights, and the milkman told us off for using the road and holding up the traffic.

'You should be on the pavement! It's against the law,' screamed the milkman.

'Don't talk to me about the law!' shouted Mr Leithen. 'I'm a retired High Court judge. I'm perfectly within my rights on this road. Since you clearly know *nothing* about the law, you'd better take this.' He handed the man his business card. 'If you're ever in legal trouble, give me a call,' he said.

We puttered along the bypass while the cars tore past us. The sun dipped towards the hills and I thought, Somewhere behind me the moon will be rising, pulling the tide up the bay.

There were roadworks on the Castle Douglas turn-off, so we left the road and bumped along on the grass verge. It was the only time we overtook anything. That's when I had my idea.

There was a caravan stuck in the traffic jam. What if it was going to Rumblecairn Bay? No. How could you know? We trundled on. The driver of the car that was pulling it was on his phone. There was a sticker on his back window: 'I've been Rumbled! at Rumblecairn Bay Caravan Site.'

I reached past Mr Leithen and pulled on the brake. 'What are you doing? I'm the driver!'

I shushed him and told him to follow me. I tried to make it look as though we were just out for a stroll.

'Don't look at that caravan,' I whispered. 'Don't even give it a glance.'

We went right past it, but then at the last moment I twirled around, wrenched open the caravan door and stepped inside.

When I turned to close the door I found that Mr Leithen was trying to follow me.

'No, no,' I hissed. 'You can go back to Shangri-La. On your scooter.'

'Once you've left Shangri-La,' he said, 'there's no going back. This is cosy.' He headed straight for the kitchenette. 'I think you may well find this little adventure will lead you into legal troubles. You're probably going to find my advice and expertise invaluable. Oh – a kettle! Be a good lad and fix us a brew. We're off.'

Mr Leithen really did make himself at home in that caravan. He helped himself to biscuits, tucked himself up in the bed and read a magazine about camping.

I found a little pull-down couch under the window. I sat there watching the hills and farms go by behind the net curtains. Just hoping that this caravan was really going to the bay today and that we weren't going to find ourselves on the boat to Ireland.

Then out of nowhere the wonky tower of the Coo Palace rose up above the treetops. As we twisted through the lanes towards it, it seemed to be turning round to face towards the caravan, as if it was pleased to see us.

Geese were honking just above our heads.

The caravan started rocking from side to side. We were on that little lane that runs along the Merse edge. We were moving slowly now. I eased open the caravan door, looked back at Mr Leithen. He gave me a thumbs-up and I jumped.

The caravan was going faster than I thought. My legs landed ages before the rest of me. I rolled down through the long wet grass.

27.
The Sea Chest

I lay for a moment looking up at the clouds, getting my breath back, feeling glad I was still alive. Then I remembered my mission.

The first thing I saw when I got to my feet was a red mobility scooter wedged into one of the little creeks, its back wheels up in the air, its front end caked in mud.

'Grandad!'

I searched all around the wrecked scooter in case he'd fallen off into the mud. No footprints even. No sign. Well, no sign of Grandad. There was a big sign. It said: 'Danger of Drowning! Fast Incoming Currents!' There was also a thick straight line gouged into the mud right next to it, as though someone had just dragged a fridge out to sea.

No, not a fridge.

A sea chest.

I looked out over the Merse, to where the trail was headed. The sun bounced so brightly off the mud, it was like looking into a headlight.

Half past two.

Already, somewhere out there, the tide was coming in.

I trudged along the track in the mud, looking left and right for some sign of him. I suppose that's why I didn't notice the big hank of blue rope under my feet. I tripped and went flat on my face in the mud. I looked up. Everything looked different from down there. The mountains were in the dazzle, but you could see clearly across the ground. I saw the long-legged wader birds dashing all over the place. I saw the salmon poles standing over to my left like a row of policemen. I saw barnacled rocks sticking up. And I saw a figure. A man walking, hunched forward, dragging a heavy box after him. He was heading straight out to sea.

'Grandad!' I jumped up.

As I stood up, I noticed something happening under my feet. Where I'd landed, I'd made a hole in the mud. As soon as I stepped out of it, water began to trickle in. Just a trickle, but a steady trickle. A trickle that wasn't stopping.

The sea was coming.

I ran over the mud, bent double so I could keep out of the glare, calling, stumbling, slipping, shouting, 'Grandad! Grandad!' The closer I got to him, the clearer I could see the danger. Every little rivulet and indentation, every footprint I made, was filling up with water. Water spilled over on to the flat mud. A skin of water was spreading all over it, catching the light. It was water that made the Merse so hard to look at. The whole bay was just one big bathtub that minute by minute was getting fuller and fuller.

'GRANDAD!!!' He turned. I thought he was going to stop, but he was only changing direction, veering off towards the left.

Then he stopped. Looked round. He shouted back at me, 'Come on! We're going to miss it!' He carried on walking, quicker than ever, further and further out.

I caught up with him. While I was trying to get my breath he said, 'Good lad. I knew you'd come. I was hoping you would. This thing is really heavy. Do you want to pull it for a bit?'

'Grandad, the tide is coming in.'

'Well, I know that. How could my ship come in, if the tide wasn't?'

'We'll be drowned, Grandad. We've got to go back.'

'I've sailed the Seven Seas with criminals and kings and never drowned once. The jetty is just there.' He walked on. 'The thing is,' he said, 'I remembered something.'

What did he remember? Me? My name?

'For ages, when it was high tide, I used to go out to meet my ship. It was never there. Then today I remembered. The ship doesn't come in at Dumfries. There's not even a jetty at Dumfries. It comes in here. Look. There's the jetty.'

The old jetty was a few hundred yards ahead of us. Little waves were already splashing white around it. But maybe if we got to it we could clamber up or at least hold on or something. I tugged at the trunk. It wasn't as heavy as I thought it would be. I tried to hurry, to beat the tide. If I just did what he wanted – but faster – we might still be all right.

Then we hit the creek. A gurgling brown current snaked between us and any kind of safety.

'No help for it,' said Grandad, striding straight into the water. 'Don't want to miss the boat.'

'No, Grandad, please, you'll get cold.' If he gets cold, he could get really sick because he's old. He trudged through the stream. I dragged the box after me. The water hurried past my legs. Even though it was only a few inches deep, I could feel the force of it tugging at me. How hard would it be pushing us when it was up to our waists? I sludged out of the water up on to the mud.

But the sea chest didn't.

It tipped backwards and stuck its end up like a shopping trolley in a canal.

'Careful there!' shouted Grandad. 'You've run aground!'

'Careful?! We're going to drown.'

'Haul her down, boys, she'll come out. We'll get her afloat again.'

'We have to leave it.'

'We can't beach her. All my rememberings are stowed in her.'

'It's not rememberings, it's memories. How can you have memories in there? You don't even know who I am.'

'You're Preston Mellows, my grandson. Middle name: Arthur. Birthday: 26 May. You've just started at Dumfries Academy. You've got very good manners and the makings of a decent cook. You fancy yourself as a bit of an electrician but you're not really. Anything else?'

I stared at him. I wanted to hug him. I would've jumped up and down but I was worried that I'd sink in the mud. I'd started to think he'd never recognize me again. The way he said it, it sounded like he was just remembering it. Like all his memories were coming back.

Then Grandad said, 'It was you. You used to come with me when the tide was high and tell me that I'd just missed my boat.'

'And then we'd go for chips and eat them in the park.'

'You knew. You knew there was no ship really. You were just being nice.'

Watching his face as some of his memories came back was like watching someone walk towards you out of the mist. First they're just a shape, and then there's colours and a face and expressions and everything.

'You learned that trick from me.'

'What trick?'

'When you were little I did the same thing to you. When your mum went, I didn't know what to do with a little one. I used to take you for walks around the city and tell you we'd been to all kinds of places, been on all kinds of adventures. I even drew you a map.'

I pulled the map out of my pocket. 'It's here!' I said. 'Look. I kept it.' I held up the Map of the World that was really just a map of Dumfries.

'Aye, that's it.'

'So I've never really been to any of those places? The Amazon? The Taj Mahal?'

'No. Furthest you've ever been is Stramoddie.'

'Oh.'

'You've still got all those things ahead of you. You can tick them off the list. Got it all to look forward to.'

'Not if we don't get moving, I haven't. We'd better get going.'

As I said that a massive wave crashed against the jetty. White foam exploded into the air. We were never going to make it there.

I looked in the opposite direction, towards the shore. Waves were scything low across the beach, breaking over the rocks and shattering around the salmon poles. We couldn't go that way.

I looked back the way we came. The creek had burst its banks now. The sea chest was half hidden in swirls of water.

We couldn't go that way either.

We were stranded. On a mud bank. A mud bank

about the size of a caravan. But getting smaller every minute as the water got higher.

All I'd done was try to look after him. But somehow I'd made everything worse. Before I came, one person was going to drown. Now, thanks to me, two people were going to drown and one of them was me. Just like when Sputnik set out to look after me and ended up putting the planet in danger.

I wasn't thinking about the planet now. I was just thinking about Grandad.

Grandad, though, was just thinking about his sea chest. He was tugging at it and pulling at it, slipping about, trying to get a grip on it.

'Grandad, stop! There's no point!'

'It floats,' he said. 'If we can just dislodge it, we could hang on to it. Maybe we could stand on it. Then when my ship comes by, they'll spy us and pick us up. Give us a tot of rum.'

I didn't bother saying that there wasn't going to be a ship or that I was too young to drink rum. I just said, 'Good idea,' got down in the water and pulled while he pushed. The chest tottered over and splatted into the mud. We clambered up on top. As we did, his harmonica dropped out of my pocket.

'That's mine,' he said, picking it up. 'What are you doing with that?'

'Someone stole it. Then they gave it back. I was going to give it to you.'

He put it in his mouth and played a tune. I'd listened so often to Sputnik making it sound like a chicken being strangled that I'd forgotten that it played music. The notes drifted over the water and mixed with the sound of the waves and the splashes and gulls. 'Fly Me to the Moon', the tune was called. He used to play it all the time. I'd forgotten. Oh, that's funny, I thought. I forget things too. I sang along while he played and the sea drummed on the sea chest. And I thought, Well, what else can we do?

Grandad was the first to see it. He nudged me

with his elbow and nodded towards the shore but didn't stop playing. A plume of white foam was speeding towards us across the bay, a V of ripples spreading out behind it as though the sea was a big brown anorak that was unzipping. Its engines whined and gurgled. The faster Grandad played, the faster it seemed to move. The engines stopped.

There, bobbing up and down on the waves, on what looked suspiciously like a mobility scooter, was Sputnik.

'So *that*'s what a harmonica's supposed to sound like,' he said. 'I told you it should be on the list!'

'Sputnik!'

'Who knew these things had hydrofoils?' he yelled.

'Mobility scooters don't have hydrofoils.'

'Oh yes, they do. It's all in the manual, which was safely stowed under the driving seat. Unopened of course. Why does no one ever read the manual?'

He looked at Grandad and said, 'Grandad, it's an honour to meet you. I'm sorry I didn't recognize you last time we met. But I know better now. I've got a message for you, from an old friend.' He sat up in the seat and he saluted. And – maybe it was the light, maybe I had salty water in my eyes – but just for a second, as his arm went up to his forehead, he looked just like a scruffy little dog, but a scruffy little dog in a space helmet.

'Laika!' shouted Grandad.

'She said you'd remember,' said Sputnik.

'Oh, I remember,' said Grandad.

'Climb aboard while I hold her steady. We'll soon have you back on dry land.'

'I'm not going anywhere without my sea chest.'

'Of course,' said Sputnik. 'I'm agog to find out what's inside that. Prez, jump off the chest.'

I stepped off. The water was up to my middle now. I helped Grandad get up behind Sputnik, and he pulled and I pushed and together we managed to heave the chest up on to the scooter. As we got it into place, it slipped and the lid flew open.

'Shut it! Quick!' shouted Grandad. 'All my rememberings will blow away.'

That's when I saw what Grandad had in his sea chest. I'm not sure what I expected. Maybe clothes or ornaments or gadgets that he'd collected on his travels. But that's not what was in there. The reason that the chest was so surprisingly light was that it was full to the top with yellow Post-it notes, all covered in lists. Lists in my handwriting. All the reminders I'd written for him over the years were there in that chest. I could see words like 'Tuesday' and 'Dentist' and some of the last Post-it notes I wrote, that had things like 'Prez is your grandson' and 'You live in Dumfries' written on them, from when he was getting really mixed up.

Rememberings.

'All my days are in there,' said Grandad, 'all my days with Prez. When I was losing my mind and he was trying to keep it for me. Like a good sailor bailing out a leaky boat.'

Sputnik stared. I thought he was going to be angry. I'd sort of made him think it might be full of treasure. Not old Post-it notes.

'I wanted to remember that he'd tried,' said

Grandad. 'Even if I didn't remember what actually happened.'

'That,' said Sputnik, 'is the most amazing thing ever.' He took out the notebook and went to write something. Then he paused. 'What do you call it?' he said.

'Post-it notes.'

'Not the notes. The thing. The thing that made you do them?'

'A pen?'

'No. The knot. The knot that ties you two together even right out here on the Merse where there is Danger of Drowning from Fast Incoming Currents.'

'Oh. That.' I tried to think of all the things that made me try and help Grandad. Being scared of losing him. Wanting him not to change. Wanting to make sure he was all right. Wanting to make him laugh. Wanting to laugh with him. Wanting that feeling I got when we laughed together. The feeling of home. Wanting that feeling back. Wanting home.

'I don't know. I don't think there's a word for that kind of knot. Maybe just being human.'

'I'll think it over,' said Sputnik. 'Let you know next time I see you.'

He started up the engine and nudged the scooter round, spraying water in my face.

'Hey. Wait for me!' I yelled.

'No room, sorry,' said Sputnik.

'But aren't you supposed to be looking after me?'

'Och, there was a right chuffing mix-up there. Turns out it was your grandad I was supposed to be looking after all the time.'

'But . . .'

'You'll be fine. It's only up to your chest. Don't try to swim it. Just keep walking. Stay calm. Careful where you put your feet. If you feel the floor giving way, swim. Good luck.' He revved the engine, spraying water all over me again. Then he turned it down until it was idling. 'Nearly forgot. Laika asked me to give you this.'

He reached into his backpack.

'Have to make sure that my seat belt's fastened first. This present is all that was keeping me on the ground in this gravity.'

He tightened his seat belt, then out of his backpack he pulled the old rubber ball with the toothmarks that he had shown me that first night.

'That's lovely,' said Grandad. 'I used to play fetch with her.'

'I know. She remembers,' said Sputnik.

I said, 'Is that the ball you used to play with her?'

'This? A rubber ball? No!' laughed Sputnik. 'This is my planet. After shrinking.'

I could see now that it wasn't a rubber ball at all. It was floating just above the palm of his hand, spinning like a little bonsai planet. The things that I'd thought were toothmarks were actually tiny mountain ranges. The red swirled about like a pocket sea.

'I'm up to my neck in cold water,' I shivered. 'If there was any chance of a lift . . .'

He ignored me. 'Prez will tell you,' Sputnik said to Grandad, 'I don't normally play fetch, but if you were to throw this, I'd make an exception. It'd be an honour to play fetch with Grandad Mellows.'

He handed the little ball to Grandad. As Grandad took hold of it he gave a yelp of pain and pulled his hand away as if it had burned him. The ball hit the water with a massive splash and a wave that rocked me back out to sea, yards away.

'Should've mentioned,' said Sputnik, 'although it's shrunk, it still weighs the same as it did when millions of us lived on it. Gravity is different inside my backpack.'

The waves surged around us.

'Has it sunk to the bottom?' yelled Grandad. 'I wouldn't want to lose your home planet.'

'To the bottom, through the bottom, down into the crust of the Earth. Maybe it'll make a hole right through your planet. How annoying is that? I came here to save your planet, and now it looks like I've made a big hole in it. There's probably going to be a tidal wave now. Sorry for any inconvenience.'

There was a terrible sucking sound and water rushed past me. As if the water in the bay was pouring into the hole that the bonsai planet had made like it was some kind of turbo-charged plughole. I saw the mobility scooter whirl around and shoot forward.

I don't really remember too much of what happened next, except that one minute I was deep in dark water, the next I was lying flat on my back on the dunes.

When I came to, I trudged up the dunes. The massive waves had flung seaweed over all the caravans. Mr Leithen was standing outside one of them accusing the owners of trying to kidnap him.

'But we didn't know you were in there! How did you get in there? You must have been trespassing.'

'Don't throw legal words at me,' he said. 'I'm a High Court judge. Retired.'

Further up, tangled in seaweed and sideways in the grass, I found Grandad and Sputnik, laughing and chatting.

'I waited. To say goodbye,' said Sputnik. 'Goodbye.'

He took off his leather collar and handed it to me. 'That's not mine,' he said. Then he undid his safety belt. The moment he did that, he started to float. A little breeze caught him and he started to drift away like a cloud.

I ran after him, shouting, 'Is this it? Is the planet about to shrink? What do I do now?'

'No,' said Sputnik. 'I found the tenth thing for the list. It was that knot.'

'What knot?'

'Home. You got home all wrong. You're a temporary kid looking for a permanent home. You were looking in the wrong place all the time. I told you, architecture is boring. Home isn't a building. People leave buildings. Buildings fall down. Even Stramoddie will change. Ray will move out and go travelling and it will be a different place. Planets shrink. Suns explode. Planets come and planets go.

Home isn't a place on a map. Home isn't the place you come from. It's the place you're heading to. All the times you ever felt at home – they're just marks on the map, helping you to find your way there.'

'You can't just leave me. I'll be on my own.'

'I told you. I'm a comet. I go round and come back again with my glove on the other hand.'

'But that'll take forever. Millions of years.'

'Time isn't a straight line. Also dog years are different from human years. Everyone knows that.'

'Sputnik, please—'

'It's like this. You go off on an adventure. Then you come home. Right? Well that's what the universe is doing now. Ever since the Big Bang, it's been heading off into the unknown on its adventure. But the day will come when it will all go back to the beginning. Everything will come home. Everything that was broken will be fixed. Everything that was forgotten will be remembered. It'll be like the biggest reverse dynamite explosion ever. And then we'll all be back together and we'll be home again.'

'But until then—'

'Here. Catch. Souvenir.'

He threw me his notebook. It fluttered down like a red bird.

– Don't you need it? To save the Earth?

'No, no. It's all in here now.' He pointed to his head. 'And in here.' He pointed to his heart. 'Pay particular careful attention to number ten.'

There was no point shouting any more. He was already too high to hear. And he kept getting higher and higher. I followed him, looking up at him, not looking where I was going. By the time he was a tiny black dot, I was way out in the bay again. On my own.

I turned back to the shore. Two big shapes were coming towards me. It was Jessie and the dad. They were riding on the ponies. The hoofs made little bright splashes as they came. Their bridles jingled.

'We were up the Coo Palace tower,' said the dad, 'when we heard a lot of barking and shouting. We thought it might be Sputnik.'

He helped me up into the saddle in front of him. First time I'd ever been on a horse. When we got down, Jessie saw what I was holding in my hand. The dog collar with the old brass tag she'd fastened on Sputnik.

'Where is he? What happened?'

Where could I start to answer that question?

Luckily I didn't have to just then. Jessie and the dad were fairly surprised to see Grandad sitting on the wreck of a mobility scooter up in the dunes. They helped us find his sea chest too.

We all went and sat by the fire at Stramoddie to get dried out.

When we were dry I sneaked up to Jessie's room and got that scrapbook *Dogs of the Future*. I showed it to the dad.

He flicked through it and said, 'You two really did want a dog, didn't you? There's even a prayer in here to St Roch, patron saint of dogs, asking him to send you one.'

'What a rubbish saint he turned out to be.'

'We'll have to give it some thought.'

Jessie rang the Temporary two days later and told me that a spaniel had just turned up in the farmyard. A bit later a fat bloke with a walking stick had come over from the caravan site looking for him. The dad had asked him in for a cup of tea. The man had started saying how his dog had been acting strangely all summer.

After a while the dad had said, 'Well, beasts like

to have their own say in things . . .'

'Figaro used to be such a happy dog, but now he seems discontented. He seems to be making himself at home here though.'

'Well, if you wanted to leave him here with us,' the dad had said, 'he'd be more than welcome. We miss having a dog about the place.'

Grandad went back to Shangri-La. I went back to the Temporary. But I visited him a lot. And he visited us a lot. He even cooked sometimes. And sometimes at weekends we both went down to Stramoddie.

'Come on,' said Jessie, 'you have to tell me. It's not fair going quiet again now.'

She was right, but it was a long story. So that's what this is. It's my rememberings.

Sputnik had said that people didn't have manuals and you couldn't really fix them. But I remembered his reverse dynamite and how the bits of an ancient wall flew back together and made everything seem new. So whenever Grandad got confused I acted like reverse dynamite. I'd pick up some of the Post-it notes and remind him what they were all about. Sometimes he remembered. Sometimes he didn't.

He liked to look at the map of the World-in-Dumfries.

'Remember you've never been to any of these places. You have to promise me you'll get to them all one day,' he'd say. Then he'd forget where he was and who I was and he'd chat about them like we'd been there together.

'Remember the time we were just leaving Murmansk and we saw that iceberg?' he'd say. 'As the ship turned away I threw my torch at it and it caught in a crevice in the ice. Lit up the whole iceberg from inside. Like a Christmas decoration. Made it easier for other ships as long as the battery lasted. And crivens it was beautiful. We all stood on the deck and watched until it was out of sight. It looked like a floating sunset. Remember?'

'No,' I'd say, 'I've got all that to come.'

The list Grandad liked the best though wasn't one of mine at all. It was that first page of Sputnik's red notebook. Every single thing on the list made him remember some story . . .

1. TV Remote – That's the only control I've got in Shangri-La. He who has the remote rules the day room. I always make sure it's me.

2. High-Vis jackets – We all wore them on board ship. When you were on your own up on deck, there was no nicer sight than another high-vis jacket coming towards you out of the dark and the wet. It meant your watch was over.

3. The Atmosphere – Sometimes clouds were all you'd have for company up on deck. You'd sit there and they'd seem to talk to you.

4. The Tide – I used to measure my life in tides, Prez. High tide was always time to go off on an adventure.

5. Eggs and Chickens – When I was in Russia they gave me a beautiful egg all painted with red enamel. That's what they do at Easter there. True. Look it up.

6. The Harmonica – Oh yes. Pass it to me. I'll play us a tune.

7. Concealer – Isn't that to do with women's make-up? Your grandma had drawers full of the stuff. They were all a mystery to me. The biggest mystery was why she thought she needed them at all. Lovely-looking woman. You're the double of her.

8. Mooring Hitch Knot – Now that is a knot, isn't it? A knot that stops you drifting out to

sea. A knot that helps you drift off to sleep.

9. Fish and Chips Outside – Remember after our big walks we'd get a bag of chips and eat them in Station Park with the sun coming down across the trees? And you could hear the weir roaring. You had to eat the chips before the seagulls got wind of the vinegar and came bothering us.

'But that's only nine things,' I said. 'He was supposed to find ten to save the planet.'

Sputnik had said 'home' was going on the list. I wondered why he'd changed his mind. Maybe he couldn't figure out what home was after all – it wasn't Traquair Gardens or Stramoddie because we didn't live there any more. It wasn't the Temporary because that was, well, temporary. But then, the whole planet was temporary. Maybe the whole planet was home.

'Home is wherever we're together,' said Grandad. Which surprised me because I hadn't said any of this out loud. He'd just read my thoughts like Sputnik. 'What's written on the Post-it note?'

There was a Post-it note stuck to the bottom of the page, with the number ten written on it. Nothing else.

10.

'It's blank,' I said. 'There's nothing written on it. That's weird. He definitely said to look out for number ten. Maybe it's blank because some things don't fit into words.'

That's what I said. I was thinking, though, Maybe it's not just rememberings, maybe it's blank to leave a space for all the things I've yet to see and do, the places I've yet to go, before the reverse dynamite goes off and all the stars start to run backwards and Sputnik – my companion – comes flying home to me.

'I don't think so,' said Grandad. 'I think Post-it notes are the tenth thing. The thing you need to pay particular careful attention to. Think about it. All my days are there on those Post-it notes. All my rememberings. All the days I spent with you.'

Author Note

The Russian word 'Sputnik' means 'companion' in English. It was the name the great space engineer Sergei Korolev gave to the first ever satellite, which he sent into orbit in October 1957. Sputnik 1 was a shiny metal football that went round and round the Earth, keeping it company with a little beeping noise, like a squeaky wee moon.

Sputnik 2 had a passenger.

It was a little dog called Kudryavka (Curly). Scientists had found her wandering the cold winter streets of Moscow. They'd taken her in, fed her, looked after her, filmed her and trained her to do a few little jobs. She was gentle and quick to learn. On 3 November 1957 they changed her name to Laika, put her inside the shiny metal football and shot her into space. She's the most famous dog in history, the first living creature ever to orbit the Earth. Everyone had heard of her (everyone called her Muttnik). Everyone hoped and prayed that she would come back alive.

But she never did.

But all the best stories start with 'Wouldn't it be great if . . .' and for years I always wondered, 'What if someone up there found Laika?'

I usually think about and plan my books for ages. But the idea for this one just popped into my head one day when I was driving along the Formby bypass with my daughter. It just jumped into the car while we were at the traffic lights, like a little lost dog looking for a home.

I took the idea back to my house, played with it, fed it and it rocketed me off to all kinds of unexpected places. I had no idea where Sputnik was going to take me and sometimes I'd wake up, crying, 'Where am I?!' Then the same trusty people as ever made up a search party to bring me back to Earth . . . namely my courageous and amazing editor, Sarah Dudman, and my three brightly blazing critics – my children Heloise and Xavier, and my wife, Denise. I'd also like to thank Venetia Gosling for letting us set out without a map. And, of course, the mighty Steve Lenton for bringing it all to life.

By the way, it's really true about gravity travelling in waves. Einstein told us this a hundred years ago, but no one was really sure until they were actually detected for the first time by the Laser Interferometer Gravitational-Wave Observatory (LIGO) while I was writing this book. We live in a surfing universe!

About the Author

Frank Cottrell-Boyce is an award-winning author and screenwriter. *Millions*, his debut children's novel, won the CILIP Carnegie Medal. His books have been shortlisted for a multitude of prizes, including the Guardian Children's Fiction Prize, the Whitbread Children's Fiction Award (now the Costa Book Award), the Roald Dahl Funny Prize and the Blue Peter Book Award.

Frank is a judge for the BBC Radio 2 500 Words competition and, along with Danny Boyle, devised the Opening Ceremony for the London 2012 Olympics. He lives on Merseyside with his family.

About the Illustrator

Steven Lenton is based in Brighton and loves to illustrate books, filling them with charming, fun characters that really capture children's imaginations. As well as illustrating Frank Cottrell-Boyce's multi-award winning books, he is the illustrator of the bestselling and award-winning Shifty McGifty and Slippery Sam series. Steven also illustrates the Nothing To See Here Hotel series, the first of which won the Sainsbury's Children's Fiction Book Award 2018.

StevenLenton.com

Turn the page for an exclusive extract from

Frank Cottrell-Boyce

RUNAWAY ROBOT

I'm part human, part machine.

I'm a bit bionic.

I'm like Wolverine.

You could call me Alfie Wolverine.

That's not true by the way. Not going to lie, I'm not even one bit like Wolverine. 'I'm like Wolverine' is one of the things they teach you to say at Limb Lab during New Limb New Life lessons. They worry people will laugh at you or start hating on you for being part-mechanical so they teach you a load of jokes and put-downs.

And in case the jokes don't work, they teach you karate.

They even teach you what to think.

For instance, don't think too much about how your accident happened. Accidents happen. End of. Start talking about it and you'll start thinking about it. Start thinking about it and you'll soon be thinking bad thoughts, such as – was it my fault? Why didn't I just . . . etc.

Talk about something else.

So I will . . .

Eric is missing.

We've searched the entire Skyways Housing

Estate and there is no sign of him. Weird, because normally wherever Eric goes he leaves plenty of signs.

For instance:

Broken doors

Crushed wheelie bins

And, one time, a car stuck up a tree.

(Controversial!)

Today there is nothing.

No clue.

It's like he's evaporated.

It is not like he is easy to miss:

Eric is 6'6"

He likes to sing

He's super-polite

He does as he's told

When he's cheerful, his eyes light up. Literally

When he's worried he spits fire. Literally

Eric tends to take things literally

He can prepare light snacks

Get rid of unwanted guests

He can be conveniently stored in a shed

He is magnetic when anxious

Everyone knows him

*

No one has seen him.

The thing is, I really wanted to bring him to show you.

'Where did you last see him?' says Mum. 'Retrace your steps.'

So I'm retracing my steps. These are my steps.

STEP ONE:

If you're going to swerve school, swerve it with style. Find somewhere to swerve TO. Somewhere actually better than school. Don't spend the day squatting on a traffic island, with your bum going numb and your phone dying of boredom. Go somewhere warm and exciting with excellent facilities and free entertainment.

When I swerve school, I go to the airport.

You're probably disappointed that I swerved school at all but, seriously, keep listening.

There was just one day when I couldn't face seeing anyone.

I didn't plan to go to the airport. My only plan was mooching. I mooched up to the Circus, which is not a proper circus by the way. It's the name of a traffic island with a tree in the middle. There were no jugglers or fire-eaters to be seen, just the 10A bus waiting at the stop. Oh, and Thursday Wells and his mates lounging under the tree.

The minute they saw me, they scrambled to their feet like predators in a wildlife documentary. When it comes to mooching, the Circus is strictly Thursday Wells and friends ONLY.

I acted like I hadn't seen them and stepped onto the bus. The 10A is a driverless bus so no one was going to tell me it was time to get off. I sat back to enjoy the ride.

Five stops later we were outside the airport. That was the nearest I'd ever been to the airport, even though sometimes the planes fly so low over our house we can see the big flaps on their wings moving. You used to read me what was written on their tails. On blue days, their smoke trails write extra roads in the air over the rooftops. But I'd never been this near to the airport and I'd definitely never been inside any airport ever.

My brain said, *One does not simply walk into an airport. One needs tickets and passports and stuff.* But another voice in a different part of my head was going, *Let's see what happens.*

I walked through the door and I was in a magic kingdom.

On the bus we'd passed shops and houses and people taking the dog for a walk or pushing pushchairs. On the other side of the airport doors it was people in suits pulling little suitcases on wheels, families dressed for sunny days, people in uniform, people getting ready to fly. There was a departure board with the names of cities that I'd only ever seen on telly on it – Paris, Rome, Prague. There were places I'd never even heard of, places that sounded made up – Faro, Knock, Riga. All the ordinary things – for instance, you and school – they all felt far away and not really real. All these new places felt like they were just a step away.

Obviously if you're in Departures, you need to look as though you're going somewhere. Even if you're going nowhere. Nowhere is a big place. It's best to narrow things down. Instead of going nowhere, pick a particular destination and decide that that's the place you're not going to. That first time I decided to not go to Disney World, Florida. I got into the queue for Miami at Area C, Desk 23. Then just let myself chill. Everyone else was complaining about queueing but I was loving it – just standing there, looking at the adverts and the people coming and going and imagining myself flying off to Miami on a school day. I tried to figure out how the airport worked.

An airport is really just one big machine. It sucks people out of the city – off buses and out of cars, packs them into metal tubes and spits them into the sky. Job done.

That's Departures.

But the airport machine has two settings: Departures and Arrivals.

Departures is just stress. Everyone's hurrying to get into the right tube before it flies off.

Arrivals, though, is just chill. Arrivals is the opposite of Departures – it sucks people out of the sky and spits them back into the city.

Departures is full of people stressing and crying. Arrivals is full of people being happy and crying. They are not looking at the departure board. They are not queueing at check-ins or baggage drop. They are mostly standing around, behind a barrier, staring at a big automatic door marked Arrivals. Soon after a plane lands, people start piling through those doors, pulling their luggage after them. If the people waiting recognize the people arriving, they duck under the barrier, rush forward and hug them. A lot of people hold up signs for their Arrivals to see. Mostly they're taxi drivers with names like 'Mr Soyinka' or something on their cards. Or 'Welcome to Delegates for the International Labradoodle Lovers Convention'. Some people make special colourful signs with messages like, 'Welcome Back, Mum, we saved the washing up for you'. Once, there was a man with a sign that said 'The Love of My Life', but I don't think the love was that mutual because he was there three days running and went home alone. Another time a load of people turned up dressed as Imperial Stormtroopers with a sign that said 'Welcome to the Dark Side'.

There's a flower shop in Arrivals called *Up, Up and Bouquet* and a café called *The Many Happy Returns*. Sometimes people have just settled down to eat there when their friends or family come out of the gate. Nine times out of ten they will jump up, have a hug and forget to go back to their food. When that happens you can walk past the table and quietly minesweep handfuls of chips, or swipe one of those massive cups of Cokes. Sadly no one ever leaves crisps. Or Pringles.

The good things in life are just too portable.

The woman who runs the café wears a big badge that reads 'Feel Free to Ask About Our Meal Deal'. It's a lie. Everything about her says 'Do Not Ask Me Anything – I've Got Paninis to Heat'. You have to be careful around her. She's the kind who notices things.

Apart from Feel Free, though, Arrivals is a party. And I gatecrashed that party.

If you're going to gatecrash a party you have to know how to blend in. Otherwise people start asking you things. Like, 'Why aren't you in school?' So I made a sign of my own. Of course, I wasn't actually waiting for anyone. Clearly a sign that says, 'Not Actually Waiting for Anyone' would attract the wrong kind of attention. So that night I rooted around in the shed, found a big cardboard box – I think it had had a duvet in it once – ripped one panel off, wrote 'Welcome Home . . .' with glitter pens, then spent ages trying to think of a name to put there. If you put an ordinary name like, say, 'Kate' then you might end up with hundreds of Kates coming at you. So I didn't write 'Kate', I wrote Kate with a twist – Katja. It just popped into my head.

That, I thought, *is convincing. Unusual but convincing.* I had no idea where it came from.

Next day, I was dangling it over the barricade when Feel Free strolled by me. Her body kept striding forward – busy busy – but her head swiveled on her neck. She was noticing me. A few minutes later she came back the other way, so I noticed her.

What I noticed was the name on her badge: Katja. So the name Katja had not popped into my head from nowhere. It was *her* name. It had got into my head without my realizing it. And now she was standing in front of me, looking down at me.

'My name's Katja,' she said. 'Are you waiting for me?'

'No. A different Katja. Aunty Katja.'

'Really? And is she coming today?'

'Yeah. This flight. From Knock. Look just landed. Won't be long now . . .'

'She's a busy woman your aunty, isn't she? You were waiting for her yesterday. And the day before and last week. You've been hanging around the airport for days. Why aren't you in school?' She had grabbed my hand. I tried to slip her grip but she was definitely not going to let go.

So I did the only thing I could.

I took my hand off.

I flipped the catch on my wrist that holds my hand in place and ran off, leaving my right hand behind in her left hand. I looked back just long enough to see her staring down in horror.

She looked up in shock.

She probably didn't know my right hand was

detachable. She probably thought my arm was spurting blood and muscles. She dropped the hand as though it was blazing hot. It clanged to the floor.

'Your hand!' she shouted, 'Come back! You've dropped your hand!'

But I did not go back.

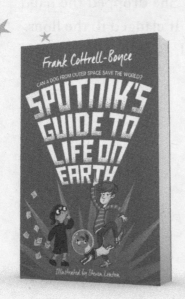

ADVENTURE!

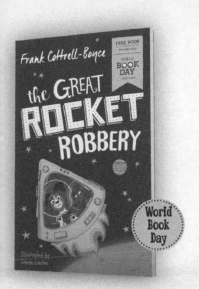

A world of possibilities